I0770628

Dedicated to my beloved sisters

Penny Cody & Cendi Baugus

From Montreal with Love

L. A. Espriux

Mask of Her Reflection in Venus

Book One

L. A. Espriux

L. A. Espriux

Print information available on this page.

Copyright @ 2023 Books by L. A.Espriux

WWW.ESPRIUX.COM

ISBN

Soft Cover   979-8-9867838-3-3

eBook   9798986783840

All Rights Reserved. No part of this book may be reproduced or transmitted in any form or by any means, electronic, or storage and retrieval systems, without permission in writing from copyright owner.

This is a work of fiction. Names, characters, places and incidents either are the product of the author's imagination or used factiously, and an resemblance to any actual person, living or dead, events, or locals is entirely coincidental.

Mask of Her Reflection in Venus
Rev. Date: 11/10/2023

Mask of Her Reflection in Venus

Cover Design & Original Artwork
by Cendi Baugus

*"So she bites into the fruit
cursed by jealousy
and slumbers in illusion..."*

L. A. Espriux

Venus Ascending

Born at equinox
Laced in season and shade
Immortal
Her eyes her mother's eyes
Winter blue
Reflecting ageless
In a glass of deception
Faded into emptiness
The promise of want
The price of enmity
And all the jewels
And all the satins
Bestowed as gifts and pleasures
All changed empty in her soul
Garment of flesh once made beauty
To be and somehow never to be
Reaching always toward illusion
Lost in depths of many eyes desired
Blood of generations mingled in her soul
Until husk of seasons withered
Harsh and brittle as her memory
Of a reflection beheld in time
Her tears now dry as desert sand
Slipping through skeletal fingers
Clutching distant thoughts of love
As when once the world
Young and lovely
So very innocent then
L. A. Espriux

Author' Personal Note to the Reader

As a female in my mind I live divided. As a male in my mind I live divided. However, the true equinox of my life comes after serving three years in the United States Marine Corps, returning from Vietnam a decorated Sergeant. This is when the *Holy Spirit* dynamically intersects my life, and I am born again. It is because of this experience that I have been provided choice to transcend meaning of male and female, recognizing the true face of both, but becoming subject to the compelling nature of neither. It is also for this same reason I am called to give testament that there greater being than witnessed through convention of mechanical process. All things designed in season, analogist to why everything here. Remembering that true knowledge is only beginning of understanding; whereas, ideological half-truths sharpened staves of calculated division. The real enemies of humankind are agents not conceived through flesh and blood. As stated in Mathew 22, verses 29 and 30, Jesus spoke these words: Jesus answered and said unto them, *"You are mistaken, not knowing the scriptures, nor the power of God. For in the resurrection they neither marry, nor are given in marriage, but are as the angels of God in heaven."* (NKJ)

L. A. Espriux

Table of Contents

1

Naked

$\mathcal{H}$e came with the wind. No one knew how long or how far he traveled. He came naked before a storm, only his bare flesh evidence that he was more than a wilderness animal. Something made less than anything supernatural. Susan Hatteras sat alone when he pawed weakly outside her door. At first she thought it a twig or a small creature scratching at the entrance. But when the door opened she sees him instead, shivering, whimpering like a fox to be let in from the cold.

Maybe it was compassion, or a thing like compassion that compels Susan to be braver than her nature. Perhaps the distance in his blue eyes softens her heart a little too much, as she thinks of the bitter cold in a blizzard that reaches out of the North Pole pawing at the eaves of her little house in the valley. So on this windy December night, Susan Hatteras allows a naked stranger from nowhere to enter her home.

He says nothing, demands nothing, but curls beside the fire and sleeps without shame. So many questions Susan wishes to ask. Like who is he, or even if he has a name, or what terrible calamity has pursued him naked to her door? So she asks nothing and only sits down silently in her rocking chair to watch him sleep in nothingness.

It is not the silence of pity. There is no pity in Susan Hatteras. She has seen the days of the great famine sweep over the land like locust devouring the living. And the children --God— *how the children suffered most!* Children that knew no evil-- their lives cut short-- cries from the past nearly forgotten now. Her own child only three, snatched away by pneumonia, and nothing she could do. There is no service, no words of comfort, even the earth too hard to break with shovel and pick. Therefore they must wait through the long winter, with only the howl of wind to console their broken souls, until finally the earth softens enough to dig a grave. She still sees in her mind the frozen face of death, the shadow of innocence that lingers and lingers inside the storage shed for five long cold months, until her heart also changes to ice. For a season she wept, and at the end of that season she never weeps again. Not even one evening three years later when Susan finds Michael slumped broken over his plow.

The land sewed with dragon's teeth in every furrow: the earth always resisting, always defying mortal hand to break it year after year beneath a hot sun. Never is there enough rain, never a cool place in the shade. Susan gathers enough strength to bury him alone. Carves out a hole in the petrified ground and lays him there beside bed of a smaller grave. Sandpaper wind stings the parchment of her face, dredging water from the dry wells of eyes faded grey. But Susan Hatteras does not cry. She has sworn never to cry again, has sworn an oath as harsh as the land, to become as it has made her. And when the last rock pounded into place, Susan is content that at least the coyotes denied their morsel. This little comfort, but enough for Susan Hatteras, enough to sustain the years of loneliness, enough to give meaning to austerity of her solitude. No longer does she expect anything more.

Susan sits in her chair rocking slowly with the same motion as the Grandfather clock ticking solemnly in the corner. It was given her by a neighbor after Michael died. It never keeps proper time, but what is the meaning of time to Susan now? It makes a noise, enough to drown out the silences. What is time anyway, except glimpse of the living moment crumpled into a finite passage of light and shadow?

This she reasoned on her own one evening just after sunset when sitting on her front porch to witness forked lightning crackle deafly upon distant horizon. It appears a phenomenon wondrous. Had this event been even a little briefer, or had she closed her eyes to the caress of an evening breeze, Susan would have missed the spectacle altogether. She remains etched forever in silence, as fire dances across the heavens. An eternity later thunder approaches, rumbling closer and closer. This is when Susan realizes the absurdity of time. Realizes how foolish dreams from the past. So Susan Hatteras forgets all she has ever known, taking a vow to remember nevermore... *before this night*.

He sleeps so perfectly still that Susan thinks he might be dead. Else a statue survived from some ancient world, gaining life only to come to her hearth, and once again change immutable. He is flawless, as always she dreamed someone like him should be flawless. Susan does not remember the dream or when she dreamed it. Only just now it becomes vivid in her mind, as a prophecy whispered into fulfillment. In the bare nakedness of this moment she desires to kiss his exposed shoulder, to know if there is feeling in stone touching stone. She imagines this only, and continues to rock slowly in her chair, as the ceiling creaks, and the wind howls down the chimney spreading flames in the fireplace.

She thinks of covering his nakedness with a quilt made during the last dynasty of her life... *but cannot.* She refuses to cover perfection, refuses to conceal that which has survived beautiful into the harshness of winter. To see the marble of his body rippled by hands of caressing shadows enough to restore her imagination. This is all that matters to her now. Tomorrow she will give him clothes once worn by her husband, but tonight she desires only to see him as he truly is. This Susan Hatteras does, and nothing more.

Shadows grow darker, an assault to smother the dying flames. Outside a blizzard has reached into the valley sculpting the land with new dimension, sweeping over the house of Susan Hatteras as magic dust escaped from a wizard's pouch. Perhaps she has slept and dreamed; or perhaps dreamed without slumber.   But when Susan looks at the place where he sleeps, she sees him sitting up and gazing into her eyes. Not the glare of animosity, for he knows no animosity or any passion that may be like it. He has sorcerer's eyes that do not blink. And he is looking through Susan Hatteras.

She is not afraid. Fear is a clinging for those who love life too little. She knows what it means to lose, to pay price of the living. As a little girl Susan remembers a Manitoba twister that tore across the Canadian South West taking her home with it. Her father nearly lost too! He manages to cling to a tree while the wind rips holes in his flesh. He was a strong man. They said that what he did impossible. But he proved them wrong. He proved what a man can do when his life at stake. He never was the same after that, as though the twister touched something more fragile inside, something he never wanted to talk about. It takes many years for the rest of that man to die.

Susan sits in her chair and remains silent. She watches his body tighten with each breath, fascinated by the exposed contour of his sleek thighs. She wants to ask if he is cold or hungry, or if he might like some hot tea. She even considers putting another log on the fire. But Susan Hatteras says nothing and does nothing.

She wishes only the silence between them. There is truth in silence. Were he to speak she would know him to be just another lie, know that he is like all the others made frail by promises at ceremonies no one understands. Her own promise forgotten so long ago... and still some part of her hopes still to remember.

It is vanity only that keeps Susan Hatteras transfixed-- not his vanity, but her own vanity. Not her own present vanity, but rather the shell of her spent existence reflected in him. She knows now the sin, prays for a way to escape the truth. But there is no escape this time-- *and she is glad!* She is glad he has come, glad that at last she is free to truly feel and remember nothing.

Susan Hatteras begins weeping for the first time in so many years. She weeps for all the beauty missed, only to find it now. She weeps for pain suffered by the hands of others— *most for the living never knowing more than life.* But what Susan weeps for in the moment she cannot say, only that it is more wonderful than anything she could have ever hoped would be.

He rises panther-like from his place on the hearth. He ascends as a fire god with burning gold hair from spent ashes. He knows; therefore does not speak. He does not need the cumbersome wrappings of half truth to cover his shame, because his nakedness is pure and without blemish. His desire transfixed in the empty space of this moment only.

It cannot be said that once he was innocent. *Rather he is innocence*. He sees clearly the weeping woman. He sees and comprehends completely the naked shame of her soul. Because he understands, he accepts, as the land accepts the snow without judgment, without resistance to that which must be.

He kneels before Susan Hatteras and kisses her softly on the lips. It is not passion that drives him. His purpose compelled by something greater than passion, something that reaches beyond the curse born of flesh and bone. A thing nameless, but with a name no one can remember. He kisses her once; and it is enough. His meaning fulfilled, he ascends a quickening shadow and steps through the open door, departing the way remembered.

Susan Hatteras says nothing, nor tries to stop him. She gives no warning that a man cannot survive naked in the snow. The blizzard has stopped now. The cold no longer matters. Nothing matters beyond this moment of his visit. Tomorrow she would ponder the meaning of the man who came naked into her house, as always tomorrow comes.

She thinks of the clock that keeps no time, the earth that bares no harvest, the merciless infinity of a parched sky. Tomorrow life would begin again for Susan Hatteras as it always begins since so many days and weeks and years. Tonight something new and extraordinary seared into presence. She remains truly at peace in her chair, eyes transfixed upon the place where he slept, the last embers dying darkly.

Joseph Moregraves awakens earlier than was his habit. The world outside transformed white and pure by ravage of a blizzard that has smothered the valley overnight. Skeleton of a Poplar tree droops wearily outside his window encrusted in an icy armor much like a man's life, soon to melt, too soon to seep quietly back into the elements.

Mask of Her Reflection in Venus

Joseph cannot say why he thought of Susan Hatteras. They have been neighbors for nearly half a century. He knew her father and her mother, and remembers Susan as a little girl. But it is only after her husband died that he really got to know Susan. She was a strong woman, a woman who asked nothing of anyone. Michael in the ground for more than a month before anyone knew she was living out there alone. So Joseph gave her a clock to help keep away the loneliness. A family heirloom handed down through the generations just for that purpose. It was slow by a half hour every two or three days. Joseph had been promising himself for weeks to drop by and make the proper adjustment, but never seemed to get around to it. This was a good morning for a walk, as good a morning as any to set things right. After all it is Christmas. What better day to visit old friends and neighbors.

An hour past sunrise, Joseph begins the mile journey to the home of Susan Hatteras deeper in the valley. Even bundled in animal skins, he cannot remember a colder day. This will later be recorded as the worst storm to hit the Manitoba west in over seventy-five years. Three quarters of a century not considered long in this kind of country, but long enough when they pass in the course of several lifetimes.

There is something not right about the house. The blizzard has piled a large snow drift on one side that rises above the windows. But there is something else odd about the scene-- *something that cannot quite be put into words.* All too quiet, too motionless, as if the house has been sleeping undisturbed for a hundred years waiting for some living soul to discover it.

Inside Joseph finds Susan Hatteras sitting in her chair beside the cold fireplace. Like the house, she seems always to have been here. She did not offer Joseph tea, nor jump up and pace the floor nervously looking for something out of place while wringing her hands, or any of the things she normally did when he arrived. She only stares blankly at a place beside the hearth, the place where he slept through her tears; the amber frozen on pallid cheeks.

No one could say why Susan Hatteras was crying, or how the door came to be open. Nor could anyone explain the bare foot prints left in the snow tracking away from the house.

Joseph Moregraves follows those prints several hundred yards through crystal halls of wooded passages. Then it begins snowing again, the trail vanished without a trace. It little matters really, since no one able to survive long a winter storm in the Red River Valley without shoes. He might find remains of the mystery visitor after spring thaw, unless discovered by some other animal first. The latter more likely, and seems therefore more just. Something else just as peculiar, Joseph finds inside the Grandfather clock a note written in longhand folded and sealed with a kiss behind the frozen pendulum.

"Bury me naked. For into this world came I swaddled in nothing, and wish to return the same back to earth."

Just after Easter Joseph takes his clock back home and buries Susan Hatteras naked in a grave according to her wishes beside her husband and child. He enshrines the place with a rough piece of slate and writes her name upon it. Maybe Joseph Moregraves performs all this so she might remember. Or else that none forget the hope and despair that marked the life and legend of Susan Hatteras.

2

The Tanner

Judith fears the dark waters-- *the shadows-- the haunting since then.* Only skeleton in the pond reminds her continually of how much things have changed. The seasons arrive and depart like the lonely sojourners which occasionally rest at her simple little house. Sometimes she offers them food and drink, and even a bed for the night. Sometimes they remain only until first light; rarely for more than a day or two. But always they went away, leaving Judith alone. Always she returns to the solitude of her thoughts. Returns to the secret reality buried beneath the black waters.

Once the pond inhabited by a variety of goldfish, by gray mountain cats, and by young frogs. Then all perished in one swift generation; and only the calcified ribs and a large v-shaped skull remains partially embedded on a pillow of reddish-green slime oozing from the bottom several inches thick. So Judith watches and waits day after day, losing concept of time and decay, as all the while the stagnant pond continues to fill with dead rotting black leaves.

There are voices in the wind. Voices that condemn and voices that promise salvation-- *voices that are completely mad!* Judith's own voice she no longer recognizes. Shades tangle on the horizon-- distant, grotesque and gruesome, changing shape in Judith's mind as the last light of each day fades into a tunnel. Always pattern of shadows the same-- always the same ghost rise out of unconsecrated graves to walk earth when the moon shines brightest.

Judith sits at evening time on the front porch beside a vacant rocking chair. If the wind blew just right, it would rock on its own. But this evening there is no wind, no stirring in the air, except for August flies and mosquitoes. He appears like a burnished spirit dissolving into existence through wavering tongues of heat. Even before he is completely formed, Judith knew him different from the usual stranger who passed her gate. She knew he had come far, had come a way not remembered, just as it was meant that he should come. Yes, at last there would be meaning to her suffering-- *at last freedom near at hand!*

"It's been a long hot day." He says, hesitating near the entrance. "Dog days like this are enough to make any animal mad! Sometimes they just roll over and die."

"Or kill...but every dog has its day. Some just die harder than others-- that's all."

"You have very pretty feet." he continues, begins to approach in stalking manner. "I like a woman bare-foot. I like your neck, too. You have a very nice shape for a woman-- very strong."

He is a man in his eyes. There is certain danger in that! Also, it means something vital, something that might save or destroy, depending on how strong. How capable of emotion he could be. This Judith senses only, but enough to cause some alarm.

"You are a stranger," she says looking straight into his eyes. "Strangers should be careful that they don't misjudge a situation too soon. Often there are unseen snares where desires lie."

He pauses and sniffs the air like all nervous animals when sensing possible threat. Then he bows his head, refusing even to look at her.

"I respect every man his property." His tone changed apologetic. "I am named Nathan. A man lives too long on the road and he forgets sometimes how to behave. It's not often that I see a pretty woman. Pretty women and names are rare when you live too long on the outside."

"There is promise or regret in a name. He had a name, a very old name, very old and from far away. You are hungry. I can see it in your eyes. Come with me, and I will give you something to eat."

Judith stands and shakes the pleats of her summer dress. It pleases the man named Nathan the way the cotton clings to her thighs. Pleases him that she wears no panties or bra, and that Judith's breast full and ripe. Nathan cannot remember when last he felt the pleasure of a woman. Yes, he likes the red in her hair, her green eyes that remind him of oceans that converge far over the horizon. He likes her lips, her nose, and the soft feminine whisper in her breathing, like the rustle of crickets in the night. He senses the things women lack within. Senses she is past her flower in age, and less concerned of consequence. With this knowledge of instinct the stranger known only as Nathan follows Judith inside.

"Do you do this often?" He asks, sitting up beside her and listening to a dull gnawing within the walls.

"Once is seldom enough; often in time too much."

Judith feels good; better than she has felt in a long time. She likes making love with a complete stranger of the night.

"What I mean to say is do you have sex with every one that passes by?"

"For a stranger you ask a lot!" She says, scratching the thick carpet like a cat sharpening her claws. "He was also a stranger. Out of the land of shadows he arrived riding upon a black horse. He came half naked, wearing only a tunic and sandals to eclipse his dark skin. There is truth in symbols of the past! He stepped beautiful as a bronze legend out of the setting sun. And the Tanner... the Tanner would be gone until morning."

"So you are married to a Tanner? Married women are all the same-- always looking for an excuse to be unfaithful. I like the way you smell. There's something special and unique about the odor of lust. It really is like something burning!"

"He also burned-- will burn forever! Always there was a devil in his eyes! Always the Tanner smelled of death! Always he came to me the same. *Please, no-- I cried-- daddy, please no!* But always it was the Tanner descended with the odor of blood and tobacco on his breath. And I thank God his pleasure quick!"

"Is your husband dead? You speak as though he might be. Are you a widow now?"

Judith stands, shakes her hair back, and straightens her dress. A single candle flickers on the floor between them, casting an aura of pulsating shadows around Judith making her look even more sensual, more subtle and young.

"I like having sex with you even if you aren't a widow;" Nathan's voice changed sly and tender.

"You may sleep here on the carpet." Judith instructs and vanishes spectrally into a fold of surrounding shadow.

Nathan rises early the next morning. He feels strong and rested, feels altogether like a different man. Over night the house had grown somehow familiar to him. He goes first into the kitchen and discovers a pot of coffee already prepared. Nathan pours himself a cup and steps through the rear exit into space of a sun-lit garden. Signs of neglect everywhere, the faint boundaries made by human design fading into barriers of encroaching weeds. For some indiscernible reason, this angers him. It angers Nathan that nature so quick to take over-- and that the pruning of a lifetime insufficient to up-root all unwanted tares.

Nathan finds Judith sunning on the stone barrier that surrounds the fish pond. She does not look up as he approaches, but continues to stare into the stygian waters. She appears in his mind a lovely sorceress gazing into depths of her magic caldron. Here she sees those events that happened secret-- special and unforgettable-- of incest, of passion, and of murder.

"It's strange to see skeleton of so large an animal in a fish pond". Nathan states sentencing, his shadow looming over her, casting even greater darkness upon the inky surface.

"Fish lived in his belly for several weeks. I watched them swim in and out, eating and swimming. First they ate his eyes, his flesh more slowly. Then one evening they were all dead and bloated. I believe that at the last they bit too deep into his heart-- released too much of the corruption all at once!"

Nathan shivers upon imagining host of watery carrion stripping away his flesh, as he lay helpless, paralyzed in death. It reminds him of what it feels trapped in the depths of oblivion without promise, until Final Day of Judgment.

"He was so beautiful, once-- like ebony-- something free and noble. Yes, an animal alive and warm-- yes, he was warm once! His eyes not like your eyes, dark and hungry. His eyes clear shedding light to my soul."

Judith drifts somewhere else in her mind. Nathan ponders briefly the meaning of her speech. She seems confused, seems to be moving through different dimensions simultaneously. Yes, it seems she is somewhere else, not fully aware of time passage or consequence of present danger. Nathan decides Judith's personality divided into more than one reality, some present others past. And in each she wrestles a demon. The things Judith truly sees in those blackened waters beyond accountability of limited imagination.

"Yes, horses are magnificent creatures. I'm certain it was a horse. I have ridden many horses in my life, but never my own. Horses have always been like spirits to me."

"*Yes...his spirit-- once he had a spirit!* At first I thought it only emptiness of my desire. *The moon will be bright tonight!* I thought that I had gone completely mad and that he was only an illusion. *They say the full moon influences the mind!* I thought so many things that I surrendered everything I had to give. *Poor him-- poor... poor him!* He was so lovely then...so lovely to touch...so complete in his soul. *Not all flesh the same flesh!* But his flesh is special like no other flesh, especially when the moon full and bright. *His love will never be untrue!*"

"I have heard it said that spirits prefer to walk during night of the full moon."

Nathan moves closer, observing the way light passes through the same dress worn on the previous night, accentuating familiar contour of her breast and shoulders, making Judith's pale neck seem longer, particularly delicate, *so easily broken.*

"I have never seen real spirits in light of the full moon, but believe they exist. I believe that all energy remains trapped for a long time. Maybe I believe that what we call spirit is actually the soul; the soul a kind of energy to make the body live. I think that the spirit is something else altogether different to reanimate the soul; either eternally alive or eternally dead. It all depends on the kind of spirit that enters into it. I believe there is but one spirit of light and many blind spirits lost in darkness. Those spirits like seeds floating in the air groping for an emptiness to receive them. I think there is something vibrantly beautiful in your soul."

She turns and stares coldly at him, lash of her green eyes never once blinking, never once revealing the truth in her thoughts. It makes Nathan uncomfortable, makes him fear that she might look too deep. Fear that Judith might glimpse some particle within his own soul he wishes to keep hidden for now.

"It's not a good thing to live too much in the past," Nathan warns, averting his eyes toward the black water. "The past is past, and there are many more dangers to be considered in the present. You should allow me to bury those bones for you."

"No-- his bones must never be moved-- *must never be disturbed!*"

"All things deserve to be buried decently."

"Never his bones-- *never should those bones be resurrected*!"

"What's so special about a horse skeleton?"

"It is a mystery why he was born mortal. He should not have come into the world that way. His eyes so pleasant, so filled with light-- *infinite*! He came as a stranger only to water his horse. *Sometimes strangers are angels in disguise!* I offered him drink and meat as well. I asked how far he had traveled, and he said too far for him to remember. I asked where he went, but he only shook his head, continuing to eat. I had never seen a black man eat before. His body was so perfect, dark like exotic wood. He said he came from the Netherlands. I said it sounded like somewhere the sun never shines and like him a place dark in my mind. He said the Netherlands a domain beyond my imagination because I had never been anywhere else except here. He promised that soon he would return there, and after a time I would follow..."

"And did he keep his promise?"

"Like you, he came from the west, except he came like a shadow riding on a black horse. The Tanner hated him for that-- hated him because his skin was dark! Hated his skin because it was without corruption, but mostly because he knew there was nothing he could do about it."

"So you made love to a black stranger and your husband found out about it!"

"You know much for one just arrived." Judith says, looking suspiciously at Nathan. "We drank the Tanner's wine and loved each other on the tanning floor. So many eyes watched from the shadows-- eyes that belonged to the Tanner. But he was gone and would not return until morning. So we allowed the wine to make us drowsy, laughed, and spoke in riddles. *His flesh was so beautiful-- smooth like ebony-- so young!* And the Tanner knew how much I desired the dark of his skin."

Nathan picks up a small rounded stone and drops it into the motionless pool. Immediately, a gray cloud issues from the bottom and begins spreading cancerously throughout.

"Don't do that!" Commands Judith harshly.

"Why not-- I don't think it's nice to talk to other people that way. I don't think I like you talking to me that way."

"Please... let him rest... let him remain as he is."

"So what happened to your black lover?"

There grows new challenge in Nathan's tone.

"I see him sometimes. When the moon is full like it will be tonight! He comes to me...loves me in a way that is special. I know his love-- *his desire for me pure.*"

Nathan grabs Judith and pulls her face toward his lips.

"I also desire you!"

"No, you mustn't-- *not here*!" Judith cries, pulling away. "He will see! He watches us even now. Always he is watching...always waiting. Come, let us go inside the house where it is safe and he cannot see!"

"Who is watching-- is it your husband or your lover?"

Judith says nothing more and departs into the house. Nathan continues for a moment to stare into the pond, which has changed completely stagnant gray by now. He then turns and follows her inside, feeling not altogether himself.

Nathan awakens beneath a net of shadows, the late afternoon light streaming through latticed windows facing east. Judith is vanished again. Again she has faded into the surrounding silence as a poltergeist of imagination. Somewhere a presence heard more conspicuous, signifying a rodent gnawing within the walls. Its days already numbered, along with the sparse furnishings that serve no apparent practical function. Squatting in the center of the room is a small oblong table simply decorated by a blank picture frame and a chipped gingham dog sitting perplexedly near the edge. Beside it slumps a worn carpeted armchair, the fabric coarse and faded, mutilated by scorch marks of multiple cigar burns. Recessed a couple of centimeters above the seat cushions, appears the laceration of a tattered incision providing easy entrance and exit for the family of rats nesting inside. There are, of course, the usual odds and ends-- sticks and rags of decorum designed to give each room a little personality of its own. But all this created for appearance sake only-- just a facade to create illusion that inhabitants of the living still here. And Nathan wonders how many more generations these rotting timbers might shelter from the elements before altogether crumbling.

He then rises from the dusty pallet on the floor and steps outside thinking that perhaps Judith again sits by the pond. The water has changed black again, the skeleton bars of a fluorescent cage forged by rays of the evening sun filtering through upper branches of a large Black Walnut tree. There was no breeze and no Judith, only the quietness of the hour.

Prehistoric dragonflies and giant striped bumblebees languish in sweltering atmosphere as primitive monsters inhabiting a lost and forgotten garden left unattended. Nathan recalls another time, a time when the garden flourished with a variety of sweet smelling flowers. When the hedges trimmed back, when the pond reflected clear and fresh. Yes, many things have indeed changed since then! Yes, almost he remembers completely! It is as though he has been here before, a recollection not altogether his own. The embodiment of something before Nathan even born that has walked the earth since beginning. It did not really surprise him that Judith lovely and alone-- that she and the house suddenly materialized out of the remote landscape like a déjà-vu dream from some obscure and frightening place in his mind. It is unimportant that Judith no longer young, nor that the days of the house numbered because of termite damage and rodent infestation. After all, time respects nothing beyond the purpose of design.

Nathan allows presence of an alien impulse to lead him along the garden path that snakes in and out of green shadows. He allows this latent presence to feel the warm sun on his face, to see through his eyes, and to know desire as once it desired.

Weeds sprout between crevices in the brick walkway as usurping adversaries bent upon annihilating every would-be kingdom of man. Part of him understands and hates nature for it. He hates the seasons which blink through a clouded lens, and the long unsearchable darkness. The garden path is all too familiar, all just as it was. Then he finds it. This is the thing sought since a long time, a thing lying in darkness, waiting for the right hand to resurrect it.

The rusting revolver wedged in the root crevice of a dead crab apple tree, nearly buried under decaying bark, partially consumed in growth of poison ivy. Five out of six of the chambers had been fired. Nathan squints because of some vague memory of pain reminding him that the sixth bullet remained intact, and that it took only five to do the job. Now the firing pin rusted solid, the mechanism useless as to its purpose. Even stranger is the feeling that another part of a tragedy remains trapped somewhere, waiting upon the hour of release. But Nathan still too strong-- *still he is able to resist.*

"You found it..." Judith says from the shadow of a tree behind him.

"It belonged to your husband-- *didn't it?"*

Nathan's tone accusing, changed sharp and brittle.

"The Tanner died as he lived. No one should escape his own violence! It is written that *all who live by the sword shall die by the sword!* I'm glad that the Tanner died by his own violence!"

"Did your black lover murder him?"

Judith does not answer, but turns and walks back toward the pond. Upon reaching circumference of the stygian border, she sits on a broken stump by the water's edge. Her eyes wide and far away, her reflection on the still black surface like a freshly painted portrait of herself before the onslaught of years bled the vital essence of her youth. This is both snare of her charm and her judgment.

"The waters were not always bitter," Judith speaks in a trance. *"Beware of wormwood which makes the waters bitter! Beware the Tanner-- he returns early and unannounced!* The Tanner knew how thirsty an animal like his could be. The Tanner knew a lot of things about animals. He knew that too much poison kills quick, too little only makes sick. But just enough will paralyze. The

Tanner learned this from his war. War is also a poison-- a poison in the soul that last and last-- *and the Tanner had altogether lost his soul*!"

"So the Tanner poisoned your lover's horse. Is this why he murdered him?"

Nathan's tone changes increasingly agitated, now condemning.

"*Poor him... poor beautiful him*... we drank the Tanner's wine and made love on the floor of the tanning shed. He was so tender...so dark...so trusting in my arms. We laughed and drank the wine and never suspected. Never knew that all the while the Tanner was watching through his many eyes. *No Papa-- please papa, no!* The Tanner took him warm from my arms so that I would always remember-- *Damn you monster! Damn you daddy! --Damn you--damn you--damn you!* "

Nathan takes Judith roughly by the shoulders and begins shaking her. For an instant it seemed she would cry, but then, her eyes change hard as alabaster, her whole body rigid. And in some sadistic part of himself, Nathan enjoys witnessing the depth of her suffering.

"So the Tanner came home early and caught you two making love?"

"No-- he will hear you!" Judith interrupts, pressing her hand to his lips.

Uncontrollably, Nathan begins licking her fingers, and then kisses her neck, biting into the exposed shoulders. He feels on fire, feels lust as he has known before. It is as though Judith something forbidden-- something always he had wanted and could never have. It is as though his desire for Judith a physical possession, making Nathan a slave to the want of her body, overpowering his natural will.

"It is nearly dark now...and he knows the moon will be full tonight."

There is an agreement of spirits within Judith, an acceptance of peace she has not felt since a long time.

Mask of Her Reflection in Venus

"You are hungry again-- *always the Tanner was hungry in his eyes, too!* Come-- he sees too much! Come, soon the moon will rise and his eyes fully open!"

Nathan follows Judith into the house. But first he turns to glimpse a velvety black current disturb the surface water that fleshes over the barely discernible v-shaped skull. This unexplained phenomenon causes Nathan to wonder if wormwood still poisoned the deeps and if more than forgetfulness rots in darkness.

This evening Nathan does not drink wine. Judith accepts him without lust, which makes his own lust even greater. He hates her for this-- hates the softness of her red hair and the bitter-sweet odor of her skin that gives nothing true in return! He hates Judith because of something mystic and secret retained always in reserve, something special and virginal beyond the hunger of his understanding.

When she thinks him asleep, Judith rises and glides wispily away. This night he follows her as in a dream he has followed her before, stealing from shadow to shadow like a lone wolf stalking unsuspecting prey, always careful to maintain a wary distance. The moon is at its equinox, as Judith steps lightly along with many other spirits of the night. She pauses briefly near edge of the pond where the incandescent bones shimmer in the silvery light of a full moon. She then continues on errant course, reaching finally the padlocked door of the tanning shed. It is no more than a small oblong building leaning noticeably to one side, where a fissure has formed, bearing witness that something below has chosen this spot to break to the surface. Judith removes something from a pocket sewn in her dress, inserts it into the lock, and goes inside. The door shuts portentously slow, followed by the click of a latch lowered into position.

Nathan approaches, peers through the clouded window, as darkness of the hour grows within him. He feels shutout and altogether bestial! He watches Judith light a candle, standing with her back turned. She then slowly unbuttons the front of her dress, deliberately swaying her hips back and forth, teasingly inching the dress up and up, until he sees completely the naked cleavage of her buttocks, the narrow ascending straightness of her back and waist. She next bends forward, allowing the garment to slide up along the shape of her shoulders and taper along her arms. Crumpling on the tanning shed floor, it changes meaningless and uninspiring; just a lump of discarded material. Judith spreads her legs apart, fully extends her body, throwing her beautiful auburn hair back, and then reaches toward the ceiling, her spread fingers graceful wings of a bird just landed.

This exercise complete, she begins to run her hands along the hips and torso, caresses the cups of her firm breasts, tracing sensuously the cones of erect nipples. Her fingers continue to explore the erogenous secrets of her own flesh unleashed, touching tenderly the contour of her long slender neck, pinching the delicate lobes of her ears, and then the quivering softness of engorged lips. But not her fingers-- his fingers! His touch as no other touch; his body made like no other body, perfect, inspiring meaning and beauty to her flesh and to her soul.

The sound of Judith's voice rises higher and higher, keeping pace with the wind rising in force outside. Judith's gaze unwavering; her eyes transfixed passionately upon flickering shadow of a black silhouette pinned prostrate against the opposite wall.

As all the while Nathan watches through the clouded window, watches as a thing shutout; hearing her screams of final ecstasy at the end, a release he never could give her.

He feels such rage-- such jealousy! He is closer to Judith than to any woman he has ever known! He tries to visualize that they experience the lust of this encounter together. That through some extremity of his own thoughts they are attached. Her eroticism changed to his eroticism, and that Judith might invite him inside. But the black silhouette against the wall blots this possibility from his imagination, as Nathan accepts in darkness the thing he must eventually do.

Judith drops to her knees exhausted and crying. She has waited long for this night and knows time grows short. She then slips back into the restriction of her dress, blows out the nearly spent candle, departing the same way she came. As for Nathan, he remains hidden in shadows panting like a rabid animal made mad by the scent of fresh blood. Something even stronger and more intoxicating whispers to him from Stygian depths of the pond.

Judith found next morning sitting on the front porch as when first he arrived. She did not even look up when he approaches, does not question what he did in the night. Nor does she question the meaning of a sack that sags heavily at his side dripping black water. Nathan moves automatically to the weathered wood rocking chair and sits down, placing the sack on the floor between them.

"Only the Tanner sits in his chair," she says, staring blankly at a distant point on the horizon. "Always in the morning, always in the evening-- since she died the Tanner would sit in his chair and never say a word. *Please, daddy, speak to me-- please, say you still love me!* But the Tanner never knew how to be close-- always his thoughts dug in her grave. Always the Tanner cursed God in his heart because she died ten years after I was born. *I love you, daddy-- I love you*! Always the Tanner far away in his heart, always he blamed me because I looked too much like her!"

"So your father was a Tanner."

There is knowledge and condemnation of final judgment in Nathan's tone.

"One night the wine coursed too strong in the Tanner's head. He came as I slept-- the stench of a beast on his hands! Yes, father was a Tanner, and always there was blood in his eyes! *No, daddy, it hurts so much-- please, it hurts-- it hurts!* He came often after that. Came, and never said anything. My father the Tanner-- *the Tanner my father*-- and when he went away to sell his skins, I prayed always that he would never come back!"

"It was dark the night the Tanner came home."

It is certain Nathan knows more than he should.

"Yes, he watched through the window in the tanning shed. The Tanner knew his wine poison. He knew it was just enough so not to kill completely, just enough to keep the soul alive. The Tanner knew how much I coveted the blackness of his flesh-- that poor man from the Netherlands-- that poor unfortunate man! *And nothing I could do to stop him!*"

"The Tanner-- you mean the Tanner."

"Yes, he was a tanner of flesh-- his beautiful, beautiful black flesh! And the Tanner knew that I was still awake and in love for the first time!"

Nathan then opens the sack, allowing something nearly round to escape. It rolls clopping across the wooden porch floor, coming to rest near Judith's exposed ankle. The skull is unmistakably human. A section of the vertebra still hinged, attached by a rubberized string of sinew, with the lower jaw gasping open. A portion of the cheekbone just below the eye socket smashed away, a second fracture near the temple, and still a third nearly obliterating the mouth, leaving only the upper front row of teeth. An irregular hole in the back of the cranial testifies to a fatal round passing through the brain in line with a splintered nose canal. It little surprises Judith that even in death still he mocks her as when alive.

"I found this at bottom of the pond covered in slime."

"You should have left him where he fell."

"You murdered your own father-- *didn't you?"*

There is no place of absolution; his tone as sound of a guillotine.

"You shot him five times with his own gun. Once in the back, once in the neck, and three times in the face-- but the sixth bullet was a dud."

"Yes-- I was glad when the monster died! He stood in the moonlight, the flash of a blade in his hand. He was amazed because there was still life in the animal-- because the poison he poured into the pond potent enough to kill ten horses. But the Tanner wanted his horses hide as another trophy. He wanted something to permanently remind me of the horrible thing he had done so that I would never do it again.

The frogs stopped singing when he stepped into the dark waters and began carving flesh with his knife, the animal too weak even to scream as the water changes to blood. But the Tanner made a mistake the night before to keep me awake when he butchered that man from the Netherlands. He should have killed me too! Instead he made me watch thinking I would take it as a lesson to never again be unfaithful to his desire. He never knew I could be so heartless. *I am, after all, daughter of a Tanner!* He never knew my hands could be so steady-- *my soul so empty!*

The moon shown bright and the Tanner was too busy cutting flesh. He turned and looked at me surprised, his eyes pitiful and evil-- *his eyes like your eyes!* And still I squeezed the trigger-- and squeezed-- and squeezed-- and squeezed!

He floated face up in the pond beside the dead horse for many days, and each morning I came to count the maggots squirm in his eyes, and then the tadpoles that ate his brain slowly. Then, one morning I came, and the Tanner was gone, vanished into the darkness of his own hell."

There is a brief pause. It is a quiet country after all; a country lost in vastness of nature's bounty. To the south-east begins wetlands of a flowering marsh, which stretches clear to open sea. A wall of mountains surrounded in a blue haze squashes all thought of discovering a clear passage north. It is a country perfumed with the poignancy of magnolia, compassed by Juniper and dark oak forests lost for miles in an Appalachian sky. Places where snake plants, poison Sumac, and Ivy slither invisibly beneath shadows unaccustomed to direct sun light. And Nathan decides then in his heart that Judith belongs forever as she is. He decides that the autumn red in her hair should never fade, that her flesh should never wither away, and that she would always remain just as she is.

"I want to see inside the tanning shed."

It is no longer Nathan's voice, no longer his eyes.

"No-- you must not! He is waiting for you. He knows. He knows who you are. Go away-- escape far from this place while there is still time-- go now, before it is too late! Please leave, and take me with you! *There is still a chance if we hurry!"*

"Not until I know what's inside."

"If you wait it will be too late! Go while there is still time-- even if you don't want me. Take food, take money, take everything-- only go quickly!"

Nathan refuses to listen. His arms strike out, one hand grabbing Judith's wrist, the other rips away the pocket sewn on her dress. The key slams with a dead thud against the darkened cranium, coming to rest under gaping extremity of the lower jaw. Judith struggles desperately to reach it, only the demon too strong-- *already his force greater than she could have imagined!*

"Daddy was a Tanner!" She screams her eyes wide with fear. "He was still alive, but the Tanner didn't care. He laid his gun on the table to use his tanning knife instead. There was blood everywhere-- *that lost man from the Netherlands!* And I had never seen the Tanner at his work before then!"

For an instant Nathan's eyes become tender. Just for an instant he is himself again. He strokes tenderly the side of her face and thinks how lovely she is, childlike, and innocent. Perhaps she was right. Perhaps he should let dead dogs lie and depart taking Judith with him. He admires how strong she is to have survived this long without the help of another soul. She is now a beautiful woman after all, with everything to offer a man in this vast wilderness of survival. Then Nathan's mind returns to vision of that silhouette pinned against the far wall of the tanning shed. *And he must know all.*

"You will be damned if you go in there!" Judith curses after him, but already he is beyond the hearing of her words.

Inside the air is pungent and oppressive, the single oblong chamber dark and foreboding even in the daytime. Several rusted tools scattered across a dust covered work table arrayed as the Tanner had left them that last time. Waves of dried blood ripple across splintered planks of a hand-hewed hard oak floor, streaming into thick hardened pools, and seeping into one corner of the uneven foundation.

A leather work apron hangs from a crude hook, the hide stiff, turned completely black. Then Nathan beholds clearly a skin like no other nailed crucified against the narrow wall rear of the oblong chamber. For the first time in his life, Nathan understands reward of this world's ultimate satisfaction-- *something only a Tanner truly able to appreciate*! Now he understands without any doubt that hides of all beasts preserve the same; and not even the grave able to claim absolute dominion. The black skin of a once human being-- *yes the outer covering of flesh only- preserved incorruptible!* The taxidermy remains hang stapled against the far partition by spikes: one in the head, two for each arm and hand, and one through both ankles of the feet.

This preserved evidence painfully macabre, searing away the veneer covering facade of human indignity. *At the same time a thing so very beautiful!* Horror changes to admiration for the Tanner who accomplished this thing.

The cowl of the face retains detail like the ghoulish features of a mask specially designed for a custom fit. Even the toenails and fingernails took such ingenious skill to be lifted seamlessly from muscle and bone. Also, the genitals and the eyelids remain supple even after so long, untouched by the withering dryness of the seasons. The only blemish on the front of the skin is a small incision about two inches wide in the side, where a knife inserted to drain the blood. And all the while something completely alien continues to grow inside Nathan-- to fill the emptiness of his being with a magnified presence no longer him.

Judith sits near the pond at evening seeing her reflection in the black water. The faded auburn of her hair combed and curled, her face washed clean, her eyes enhanced by mascara, with a touch of rouse on dry lips adding colorful contrast to the paleness of her skin.

She wears her mother's white wedding gown, the very gown which often the Tanner made her wear for his pleasure. Yes, Judith looks younger in the pond than her true years-- looks pure and spiritual, like a lost angel fading into an abyss among distant stars.

Judith is little shocked when his reflection appears behind her covered by a heinous black hood-- *his face, but not his eyes-- his flesh, but not his soul!* She is even less surprised when the waters change suddenly gray, putrid cold filling her lungs, a detached body convulsing in a dream only part real. She does not scream, does not struggle-- aware only that her salvation nearer than ever it has been before! Now at last she will be joined with the one she loves forever more. *Judith will never again fear the shadows...nor weep again.*

The Tanner sits in his chair at sunset watching patiently the road. Always he watches and waits for someone to come. Always there is darkness in the Tanner's eyes. He knows that in time someone must come. That in time all the world must pass. In his thoughts are fleeting memories, black and white, things in the tanning shed that never grow old in his mind. He thinks to hear voices in the air; and always something warm and sticky on his face. He thinks the two silhouettes against far wall in the oblong room of the tanning shed somehow alive.

Light and shadow haunt his thoughts, playing lost and seek within dark corners. And when the moon full they want to punish him! But always the Tanner is alone. Always the silence; always he sits, and watches, and waits.

3

The Dancing Ballerina

*V*ouina, the dancing ballerina, created one night from
ashes of a dream. She began as a secret, an act of love
while the world slept. No one would know the lump of clay
or the sprig of wood that became Vouina. No one would
know what colours mixed together before the paint of her
flesh added. Nor that Vouina's eyes tiny blue jewels
removed from an elegant silver watch that once belonged to
an Empress. Even her hair real, blond as corn silk,
preserved for unremembered generations in a bronze locket.
Also, her tu tu and slippers fashioned from a blue silk
handkerchief imported from distant exotic shore. Placed
upon her delicate finger a tiny gold band forged from
shavings of a wedding ring given in the past.

Source of this wonderful miracle is a mystery that perplexes the waking world next morning, as all suspect the old toy maker has gone mad at last. All think this except the younger children that wander into his toyshop. In innocence, all believe Vouina has existed always. Existed like the haunting tune born in the black wooden box beneath her feet. Like the wheels and springs of the universe suppliant to the destiny of everything.

In time one generation grows-up, and then another. Through each generation, their hearts grow dimmer as they forget. Until secretly they begin to think the toy maker blasphemous to attempt creation of an image so perfect, so nearly mortal, and so lovely that almost the mechanism seems alive. Nevertheless, they agree to overlook this small sin. Agree to forgive the old toy maker because of the many happy memories he has sewn into their existence when once they too were children. Because his toys last forever and because they fear day of his departure, when there will be no more toys. So they pray secretly in their closets, hoping that soon the toy maker might take an apprentice to whom to teach uniqueness of his skill.

Vouina dances for the youngest when asked; even dances for grown-up parents, if seldom they wish again to see. Yet, no one appreciates her more than the toy maker himself. No one heart made more alive than his own each time Vouina bows and turns round and round. Not that he forsakes the rest of his creations-- because all his toys special; all made from essence of his soul. But even he unable to deny, Vouina born from an inspiration above all the rest. She is, in some vague sense, the summit of his expression here on earth. This is also reason the toy maker's life changed empty.

One evening past midnight the toy maker puts away his tools, pushes aside the block of wood that will be a tiny wishing well. With the sureness of a wizard, he reaches under the counter and lifts veiled object painted with the moon and stars.

"Dance for me tonight, my lovely Vouina." He commands, lifting the veil. "Dance and bring me happiness!"

However, Vouina does not move, the music refusing to begin. She remains frozen at point, her slender arms raised over her elegant head in protest. The toy maker looks quietly at her for several minutes; then begins to weep. He weeps because of frustration in his dreams. Believing himself never truly loved by anyone, and because of imperfection in the world. But most he weeps for weakness in flesh and blood. Considering all his sacrifices have amounted to nothing, and now the only thing left ugly reflection of an old man never loved.

Taking a screwdriver, the toy maker carefully opens the secret reality of the music box. Meshed in one of the gears-- so tiny-- so indiscernible to any eye but his, a particle of sand wedged between the teeth.

"My poor Vouina-- it is no wonder that you will not dance!" He sniffles, and wipes his eyeglasses.

With the gentleness of a lover, he extracts the rival element. Immediately Vouina twirls into motion, spreads her arms wide, bowing at the waist, and dances to the delight of her creator. She dances like always, dances after the pattern of his design, which causes another kind of sadness in the toy maker because of something he could not give. When the music finished, he sighs heavily and restores the veil. Almost his Vouina alive-- almost his vision realized in this present. It would be ridiculous to hope for more at his age. However, that night, like every night, he and Vouina dance in a dream among distant constellations to music altogether alien to this world.

It was evening. The precise evening is unimportant, because to the toy maker days and nights come and go like wind from different points of the compass. He is sitting behind his workbench stitching a new face on a doll he had made many years before, hunched under the dim light of a sputtering candle, casting his shadow like an emaciated spider winding thread. Just then the front entrance doorbell rattles, as someone special enters his shop. He did not know this at the time. He did not know that his visitor had travelled very far, and that there more magic in his toys than even he imagined.

"Good day to you little princess," he says to the young girl, completing the last stitch with seamless imperfection.

She only gazes up at him, her eyes wide and innocent, even more blue than Vouina's eyes, somehow more perfect, which makes him envy the artisan responsible for their fashion. His Vouina was also innocent, but not in the same way. Her innocence more his own innocence, as deep inside the old toy maker fears his knowledge of the true world too great. It makes him dizzy to look too deep into those eyes, reflecting an infinity that might exist beyond the world of his toyshop.

Almost the toy maker feels himself fading away, fading into an absence of time and meaning, a moment his pain of loneliness lifted. He begins to shake with sobs of forgotten memories trapped deep within, groaning and whining like a small wounded animal. He then buries his face in his hands, as a wellspring of pent-up tears erupt from the sadness in his grey eyes. When at last the paroxysm passes, the little princess is gone. Already the world changed dark outside. Already an autumn full moon shines through the shop window, as presence of a guardian spirit watching over the sleeping world.

Each hour after this inspires new hope to the toy maker. Each day he watches from the morning until late into the evening for the return of his special visitor. Many children come and depart through the seasons. They come with their parents or with their friends. Some come alone just to look and to hope, or just to watch Vouina dance. Never is the little princess among them. Never anyone old or young, when asked, knows anything about her. Until finally the old man decides it just his imagination, accepting her visit as a dream, as he may have dreamed existence of one of his toys.

"Oh, Vouina," he laments often near tears, watching her twirl and bow; "I am a foolish old man to think that there could be anything more than you. Please forgive me my lovely Vouina -- my lovely ballerina-- forgive me for ever wishing to have anything more than the happiness you bring me now!"

And Vouina continues to turn without complaint, cast beneath the shadow of his sad eyes, as frustration of a dream destined never to be fulfilled.

One evening he is in his shop like before. He has just finished putting the last magic dab of colour on a piece of wood that instantly becomes a happy fisherman. This he adds to a special collection on a middle shelf between a circus clown and regiment of miniature soldiers standing at attention. He knows instinctively this to be the perfect place for it. Just another tacit detail manifested from the wondrous counterpane seen in his mind. Then the front door of his shop opens and closes, followed by the clatter of little feet on the wooden floor.

"Little princess!" He exclaims, unsure rather or not he should believe his own eyes.

She was guileless in every way, barefoot, and without shame. She looks upon his handiwork with pleasure, with childish satisfaction and excitement. She perceives in amazement the paper dirigibles and wooden ships suspended from the high ceiling by invisible strings. She passes over the silent generations that represent every doll ever made lined on shelves against the walls like all the homeless children collected in dark corners of the universe. Yet her eyes never rest for long on any particular object or display. Rather they seem to be searching for something special. Something she knows already there.

"What in the world are you looking for, little princess?" He demands perplexed. "You are not at all like the other children. They always ask so many questions. No, you are different in a way that is... *special.*"

"*You are better now.*"

Her voice flows into his soul like a river, wondrously clear and refreshing. He does not know if this a question, or if she has made a proclamation of healing to his tired spirit. Nevertheless, he feels instantly revived, better than he has felt since a long time. Just now he knows full measure of true feeling.

"Yes, little princess", he sighs, wiping the lens of his eyeglasses. "Yes, thank you, I feel so much better now."

She smiles approvingly, as if to say, *"Of course no one is perfect and it is good for all things to be special sometime".*

Still those marvellously clear blue eyes continue to search within every cobweb shadow for something even more important than words, more important than the sentimentality of the old man's thoughts.

"Maybe I can help you decide." Then his face brightens. "Yes, I think I know just what you are looking for!"

Jester-like, he reaches into the darkness of a corner, and raises a body into the light.

"This is Annick. She came to me one evening in much the same way as you did the first time. Annick has been waiting for so long and needs so very much to be loved by someone.... someone like you, little princess, to make her live."

The young girl takes the doll affectionately into her arms. Immediately the toy maker knows that as always he has made the proper choice. He believes deep in his heart that Annick born in the likeness of happiness unique to all his children in season.

"Annick has hair just like your hair little princess. Your hair, of course, is much longer and finer! Yet, do you not agree that there is no other doll like Annick in this whole world."

She nods her head yes, but in her eyes belies another truth made partly of wish, part her own and part the old man. Nevertheless, it makes the toy maker happy that he has found a good soul for one so special. What greater happiness matched in life than to find true love?

"Before you go away, little princess, I would like you to meet someone else also special."

He next presents the black veil painted with a white moon and stars that protects the secret of his most beloved creation.

"This is Vouina, my beautiful ballerina. Her eyes are also blue, also from a place far away. See how gracefully she dances. Vouina was born to dance this way."

He states this with particular pride, lifting the veil. The ballerina instantly raises her head, spreads her arms, and begins to dance. She hesitates, as though in recognition of the little princess. Next, she twirls clockwise, rotating as designed by the toy maker. Yet, with each turn, she pauses in front of the wide eyes of the little girl. Each bow more laboured against the hidden mechanism that manifests her mock existence. It deeply troubles the toy maker to see Vouina struggle so. He would have given her a few drops of oil, only he worries that such an act might frighten the little princess. In anticipation to his greatest fear, Vouina freezes in an awkward position, her face tilting garishly up at him.

"Poor Vouina is tired tonight," the toy maker hastily reports, wishing to cover up the mistake.

The little girl backs away, an expression of horror on her face. She looks first at Vouina, then at the toy maker. He has suddenly changed into a monster in her eyes. Now she knows the source of his unhappiness; *knows the terrible secret in all his toys*! Pressing Annick close, the little princess turns quickly and vanishes into the night.

"No, wait-- please, little princess, don't go-- not yet!"

Mask of Her Reflection in Venus

His petitions echo vainly, only emptiness of night, the streets dark and vacant, and only the stars shine visible, like host of angels waiting for a new moon to pass. The toy maker shakes his head sadly and returns into the dungeon of his shop.

Next morning he awakens earlier than his usual hour by sound of knocking at the front door.

"Good morning, sir, my name is Nicholas Claus," announces a blond youth with twinkling wintery green eyes. "I have come to be your apprentice."

"Apprentice-- I haven't advertised for an apprentice. You must have come to the wrong place."

"No sir. You are the only Toy Maker. I've come to learn all that you will teach me before... before-- well sir...it is the nature of all things to change!"

The toy maker pensively turns this idea over in his mind. True, it is the nature of all things to change. He had witnessed this phenomenon more than once during the creation of one of his toys. Yes, change inevitable: to change from one definition to another-- to change from a seed into a living tree, from a tree into a simple block of wood, and from a block of wood into a meaning potentially sublime. Why change should not continue on and on into a designed tapestry of destiny never meant to end. So starting that very morning, Nicholas, a tall lovely young man from the north, consigns to be the only apprentice to the only toy maker in the world.

Nicholas arrives early each morning at the same hour, and departs at the same hour every evening. He watches patiently the practiced skill of the old toy maker, yet so little of the art he is able to retain in his own hands. He enquires continually, but always the answers leave him even more confused.

"Since no understandable logic exists in nature;" the toy maker instructs him on more than one occasion; "then how do you expect to create anything using the logic of your understanding. Nicholas, allow the creation to come through you, don't try to create it from yourself."

But try as he might, Nicholas Claus unable to master even the simplest techniques. To him Vouina made flawless, a creation without equal under heaven. So young Nicolas worships the old man as a son committed totally to the duty of his father.

It is quite possible that Nicholas would have mastered at least some magic of the craft had it not been for the return of the little princess. Alone in his toyshop, the old man had fallen asleep on his workbench while watching Vouina dance. He did this sometimes; lately he did it more often. Upon opening his eyes, the toy maker sees her clearly; sees her unblinking blue eyes staring up at him, as passage of light connected through existence unimaginable.

"Little princess-- I thought you would never come back!"

He manages to control his excitement, to maintain tone of his voice just above a whisper, so as not to risk frightening her again. He is getting old after all, and pattern of his voice fluctuates sometimes. This, too, a sign of change, a sign that not even his toyshop might continue forever after the same fashion.

"As you can see Vouina is much better tonight. Have you come to watch her dance some more?"

A tear appears in the corner of one eye and runs down a smooth, unblemished cheek. It happens so naturally that almost the toy maker wants to ask the extraordinary mystery of her creation. Almost he would discover another secret, the secret of being without end. He had wanted to give Vouina tears, except the springs and gears that make her to move and so lifelike would have rusted solid. This singular imperfection torments him with pain at times unbearable.

"Have I said or done something to make you unhappy little princess?"

She nods her head, yes, he has.

"Then please tell me what. I am an old man-- an old foolish person insensitive at times. If ever you should grow old, then you will understand. I'm not made to last as long as my toys. It's a sad thing to be a man, little princess-- so very sad to live all days of life alone and never know full measure of what it means to be."

The expression on her face changes suddenly. How it changes he cannot say, only that it as the disturbance of a ripple in a clear pond reflecting a subtle disturbance below the surface. Vouina's flesh was not so soft or elastic. This, decides the toy maker excusable, since not all flesh the same.

"She is so lonely," states the little princess at last, never once taking her eyes from Vouina. "All your toys are so lonely. You have done such a selfish and terrible thing. It is not possible you should go and leave such emptiness in the world."

The toy maker is stunned speechless. Of course, the little princess was right. He had known it for a long time-- perhaps always! Only he refused to acknowledge the truth. He had denied always that his creations sprouted from the loneliness of his heart. That Vouina the greatest loneliness of all conceived in a night of greatest solitude, formed in the image of dream to become something surpassing anything he could accomplish. Yet, even she falls short of his vision. Yes, even Vouina lacks something vital and indescribable! He had given her everything: sight, movement, even a form of immortality. Still, the thing he could not give her has plagued his soul continually. Almost he thought to know each time he saw a cloud of birds flying south for the winter. Nearly he realised when the children came into his shop after school to watch Vouina dance. Only presence of this little princess makes him to see the ugly truth unmasked-- to see himself as truly he is. But there is a price in understanding too much! Now he wishes she had never entered his shop; wishes again to sleep once more in the sentimental illusion of self-adored pride never to awaken!

"No-- No, little princess, my toys bring much happiness into the world! What would they do without them? Think of all the little children like yourself, who would never know what it means to imagine and to feel love. What you ask is too great-- too serious a thing to be accomplished so soon!"

Even as he speaks the toy maker knows the emptiness of his words. He knows them to be vain and meaningless, just repetitious symbols to comfort a world absent of faith. This time he does not try to stop the little princess. It is the last time she would come, the last time her flawless blue eyes would pierce into the nakedness of his gifted soul.

"My poor Vouina, there is so much of the world you don't understand; so much of the music that escapes you-- escapes us both! Dance, Vouina, my lovely ballerina, dance! Tomorrow all the world will know meaning of truth through eyes of beauty unimagined."

Vouina bows and turns, lifting her hands high over her head. Within her eyes born reflection of something wondrously clear, as a transformation begins spreading through flickering shadows surrounding a nearly spent candle.

Nicholas arrives next morning at his appointed hour. He thought it odd that the door still locked, supposing that the old toy maker-- who after all was getting on in years-- had simply overslept. Using the key given him, Nicholas inserts it, turns the hasp, and steps inside.

Yes, the old toy maker had indeed gone completely mad in the end. What possessed him to do such a thing? What was the meaning of his last creation that could not possibly endure beyond a day? There was not a toy left in all the shop, not a single drop of paint or piece of wire. There is no workbench, or his carving tools, nor any singular furnishing. Not even a partition to evidence that this place once occupied. The chamber cold, swept clean and empty-- but not entirely. In the center stand two life-like figures entwined in frozen dance, which is the reason why it so cold inside. The figurines carved from a single block of ice, complete in delicate detail, magnificently bright in morning light. One is the image of Vouina, the dancing ballerina. The other very much resembles the old toy maker, as he might have looked when young, a visage intent and handsome. In their eyes sparkle of light refracted from a source not of this world. Joined together they have become greater than the elements.

Only this dissolving remnant remains, surviving miraculously until morning of the next day, and destined to finally melt in each other's arms and flow between cracks in the wooden floor to go where all water goes. Stranger still is that every toy ever made by the toy maker has simply vanished overnight. Some might suggest that thieves responsible. Few, however, actually believe this. It only seems somehow logically appealing to minds more pragmatic. Always there remains mystery of the ice sculpture that defies all natural reason.

Nicholas Claus, the toy maker's recent apprentice, managed to acquire some knowledge of the craft during his brief observation. He never would be as skilled as the original toymaker, nor would any of his toys ever approach so near to being alive. Nevertheless, Nicholas Claus continues to make toys according to his gifts. This promises enough to the world of make-believe, sufficient to inspire dreams made of more than imagination.

4

Eve of the Quiet Man

It is the eve of Hope's thirty-third birthday, when her eyes meet those of the quiet man. He sits in a dark corner at her favourite bar smoking a pipe. He seems so alone, altogether out of place-- so far removed from the flashing lights and Rock and Roll of her usual hangout. Then she recognizes him, knows immediately within herself that he is different from all the other men that have interested her.

Hope knows even then that this quiet man will receive her in a way to make her live again.

"You are English?" She enquires. "No, American."

"American-- good--I'm glad that you are American. I like the sound of English... at least... I like the language. Yes, English has a pleasant sound. But really it is you Americans that speak the words most nicely."

"Thank you. I rarely think of language like that."

Hope pauses reflectively to determine if his tone a rejection, or if he is the kind of man who ignores all women, preferring that they come first to him. Yes, this must be the case. There is too much gentleness in his presence for him to be capable of rudeness. The way his eyes glisten beneath the orb of an artificial moon suspended above the bar excites her in a way she cannot explain, something Hope can only interpret as peace of this quiet man.

"I have known at least two Americans in my life. I like the way Americans think about things --very good lovers too-- very smooth with a woman. If ever I choose to live in another country, it will be America."

"Why would you think America a better place to live?"

Hope is surprised by the bluntness of this response. First, because she did not think that really he was even listening to her. But more because she knows the emptiness of her meaning...and knows that he also knows.

The pleasantness of his accent pierces the environment as melodic syllables strum from a lovely instrument, blending with the beat of a modern tune Hope particularly likes.

"I know that America is a very large place. I've seen pictures of it only in books, but I remember reading that there are at least fifty states. Fifty states! It seems such a grand number for one country! I just always thought it might be nice to live where there must be so many people."

"All spaces become crowded when you live there long enough."

"I especially like pictures of Hawaii and California, except that I'm afraid of the sea. I hate to admit it, but I'm afraid of open spaces-- even just looking at those pictures makes me ill. No, I think America is too big for me to ever really consider living there. But American men--that is something entirely different!"

The quiet man carefully packs his pipe and adds fire, sending a cloud of smoke in the air that mystically changes into a perfect blue halo. Hope has of course seen smoke rings before, but for some reason this solitary phenomenon gives her a chill of wonder.

"You do that very well," she says with a hint of practiced naiveté. "My father once smoked a pipe. He said it was better than cigarettes. He stopped smoking altogether after he and mother divorced. Nevertheless, I envy you men how elegantly you hold a briar."

"Would you like to enjoy a puff from my pipe?"

"Heavens no-- I am just saying that there is something sexy about a man with a pipe in hand."

"I believe a woman holding a pipe could also be sexy."

"You say that now, but I know how men think. When it comes to women there is always a double standard."

Hope says this with seductive practice, but also believing wholly within herself truth of the statement.

"I think I would not mind seeing you with a pipe. Yet, I do agree there are a lot of double standards in life. Not all injustices against women only."

"Don't believe that I'm a feminist. Besides, I like my bras too much to burn them. 'Rah--Rah--E.R.A.' is big in America. I guess women in America are more politically radicalized than we are here. I think that in my country women like better to feel feminine in the arms of a man!"

Hope allows her voice to trail purposely away. She accomplishes this partially by instinct, partially by conscious design, knowing this just part of her truer nature.

"Pleasure for every man is different-- like every woman is different."

There is certain challenge in his voice, an observation that makes Hope a little uneasy.

"I think men in general are only interested in their own pleasure. It is just the fly of their nature. I believe women are traditionally far more giving-- again nature. However, some men give more than others."

"Perhaps women also snared by web of their nature, with some giving less truth to receive more the lie."

His eyes speak more than words, as they search deep into the fine crevices of her face illuminated in a flash of light from behind the bar. A secret part of Hope anguishes over what really he might see.

"I... guess... I firmly believe that everyone gives only as much as they are capable at the time." Hope exhales hesitantly. "Besides, most everyone has a unique point of view concerning matters of the heart. Everything true and not true comes from the heart."

Hope pauses and gazes deeply into the bottom of her nearly empty glass. Here another truth always she has avoided.

"Truer the heart the more easily deceived," cuts in the sound of his voice.

"Yes, perhaps you are right. Nevertheless, the real sign of character is when a person begins thinking with the heart."

"Hearts are made to break... and also to break..." he says seeing something past her.

"I would ask your sign, but I'm sure you are either a Taurus or a Pisces," Hope hastily interjects. "You could even be an Aries, except Aries people usually make me feel uncomfortable."

The quiet man refuses to acknowledge what is his true sign; only looks up at the artificial moon suspended over them, pretending not hear her.

Hope likes this about him. She likes the possibility that he is uncontrollable, and remains secretive in ways that fascinate her curiosity. Even more, Hope is intrigued by the contrast of their two fleshes. Her skin so pale without makeup, "*un vrais tache du lune,*" her mother often said. She never particularly liked this genetic characteristic, and wished always to have more skin tone. In contrast, he is as a burnished statue revived from the ruins of Mount Olympus depicted in a book Hope read while in high school. She is light and he is shadow, a mix of perfect elements to make context of a dream.

"Perhaps…you prefer to be alone. Perhaps I am talking too much. Do you think my conversation boring?"

"No, I enjoy the sound of your voice. It reminds me of another sound once I knew."

"I'm glad for that. As a woman you learn what it's like to have boring people talk to you all the time. It's a terrible feeling to be trapped by words. I would never want to make someone suffer the same."

"Where dreams sing loudest angels dance free."

Hope likes the things he says. She does not exactly comprehend the meaning, but likes it all the same. It is not so much what he says, but the way he says it. Each word carefully chosen to paint an image from his mind laced with meaning of greater importance than the spoken vocabulary only.

"Do you like music? You seem to me to be a musician. I would guess that you play a string instrument. No-- not a guitar-- everyone these days plays a guitar. I play the guitar sometimes. I sang folk songs on a T.V. show when I was just a teenager. It was a nice souvenir... I was so young, so innocent--and I made so many people laugh then! You do like to laugh don't you?"

He says nothing back, his eyes twinkling perceptively.

"Yes, I'm sure you do judging by the lines around your eyes." Hope continues. "They call those laughing lines. We women have them too. Thank God for cosmetics! Men are lucky because they don't have to worry too much about wrinkles. As I was saying, I bet you play a saxophone or a trumpet. Sensitive men usually choose wind instruments. I'm not sure why. I think because they like to create things from deep within-- like for the music to come from their soul. That makes them dangerous at times. Sensitive men like to control things."

"Do you think me dangerous?"

There is challenge in his voice.

"Everyone can be dangerous sometimes. No one really thinks this until it happens. Only then, it is too late. Only after is the pain real."

Hope states this fact through experience, as she half listens to the beat of the music in the background.

"Have you suffered because of pain?"

"Some people have more pain than others. But without pain we might as well be dead. Pain drives us to do all sorts of things. Pain is all around us, if only we open our eyes."

"Perhaps pain is all in the seeing. What pain drives you tonight?"

"That's really not fair! It's like saying you don't care. That's the trouble with the world today. People just don't care anymore. I think the generation of my mother and father different. I think they really cared for each other once. You might find that difficult to believe if you saw them together today. But I think that once they really needed each other a lot. I was married for nearly five years, but I never loved my husband really. I got pregnant with Annick-- that's my daughter-- during the first year. We lived in Paris near the Eiffel Tower. It's really not all that glamorous when you must see with the same sight each morning you awake. Annick is the only reason we stayed together for so long."

Hope pauses and takes a deep breath. It is not often she remembers so deeply, feels so acutely pain from the past.

"People sacrifice a lot of things for their children. If you have children of your own, then you know what I mean. Do you have a wife somewhere in America?"

"No."

"You're lucky --I'm not married, either-- not anymore! Marriage is a big commitment! Most people refuse to see who they're marrying until too late. I was very young. He older, but was too young in his head. In less than five years, we just gave up. I guess I am the one that surrendered first. I met a younger man through my sister. He was good with horses, good in a lot of ways... but he was also lazy. I didn't know that about him. I wouldn't have cared even if I had known! He was a gentle horseman, very gentle, and very caring. He's married now, and with a child of his own. You do like children?"

"Yes, I like horses, too."

This is exactly the response she hoped from him! Perhaps not to the letter, nevertheless, Hope knows now without any doubt that the quiet man must presently share something with her lost in her heart since a long time. In truth, maybe she only wishes this. Maybe more dream to the reality than she knew.

"Do you also see women?"

"Yes... I see you."

At last he said it. At last she has penetrated some of his mystery. Yes, he is a man-- not a spirit-- not a ghost--yes, the quiet man needs what every man needs. This disappoints Hope for some reason she does not fully comprehend. It disappoints her that this quiet man desires as she desires, and wants as much as she needs to be wanted. Because his flesh will be warm like the touch of all flesh. His eyes so calm, so deep-- so very penetrating-- and Hope has an emptiness tonight that only his presence able to fill.

"I live not far from here," she announces with a straight forwardness that surprises even her. "I was lucky to find a place in this area. Everything's so expensive now. You, being an American, probably don't notice so much. But I tell you, the economy here is not good. Still it's a safe neighbourhood. I like it because they left the trees growing along the sidewalk. Trees add something personal to one's vicinity. The strong shadow of a tree makes me feel more protected somehow. I know that probably sounds silly to you because you are a man. Men see the world differently. But I've talked to other women that feel the same way I do. They all agree that trees are special."

Hope takes a deep breath and brushes her blond hair back with red painted fingernails. It seems so natural they should leave together.

It's a pleasant walk from where I live to here. I always walk, even when it's freezing cold. It's not so very cold tonight because they predict it will snow. Do you enjoy walking at night in the snow?"

He looks at her in momentary silence, as though considering a delicate response to her bold proposal. The dark quiet in his eyes makes Hope uneasy. She feels suddenly lost and unwanted. Just when she thinks to excuse herself, the quiet man speaks softly.

"Yes, a walk would be nice. I have a bad leg. When I sit too long, it begins to get stiff. A walk will do my leg good just now."

"How did you injure your leg-- in a war? It seems America is always at war somewhere. I had a fiancée after high school, who went away to fight in a war. He didn't need to go because my country wasn't involved. We usually prefer to remain neutral, you know. Anyway he wanted to prove something to me... to himself. I ran into him years later near the meat section in the super market. He claimed not to remember anything about us. Poor fellow, I thing he also received some kind of injury on the battlefield. War must be a terrible experience."

"War is something men rarely talk about, except to each other. Even then no one tells completely the truth."

"It's too bad because women also like to know about those things. Maybe by sharing we could better know each other."

The quiet man rises from his seat and slips on his cold weather jacket. He then helps Hope snuggle into her Norwegian Fox coat given by Hope's ex-husband. It is an elegant fur that blends well with the long silk of her hair.

"Above the clouds moves shimmer of a full moon through stifled heaven." He says, as they stroll along the empty sidewalk.

"That's lovely, but what does it mean?"

"It means you look particularly beautiful in moonlight, as a white fox lost in snow."

This is an odd statement in Hope's mind. Brightness of the moon scarcely visible behind thickening clouds, as begins large flakes snowing out of the east. The pale presence of the lunar body nearly devoured into nadir of northern night.

Instinctively, he chooses the right direction to Hope's dwelling. There is no hurry in his steps, no indication that he considers the hour late, or that his expectations more than the patient solitude of this moment. Hope marvels at the calm in eyes of the quiet man. Marvels his strong body--but mostly because this night he has chosen to spend with her.

"I hope you don't mind if I hold on to you," she says, clutching his arm after nearly slipping. "It's not easy to walk on ice wearing boots with high heels. The things a woman must suffer to please a man!"

"To be a man is not without challenge."

"Yes, but really it isn't the same. Your legs are almost never cold. Just imagine how much pain your injured leg would suffer if you had to wear three-inch heels every day in the office. No-- you men really don't appreciate just how lucky you are!"

"There's a lot of advantage, and a lot of disadvantage-- it all depends on your point of view. Of course, if all were the same, just think how unproductive life would be. Contrast is what makes the passage interesting. There is certain reward even in things less convenient."

It amazes Hope that this quiet man comprehends so well, and how uncomplicated he makes everything seem. They continue to walk for several minutes, speaking to each other only occasionally, preferring more the silence. Hope usually did not like silence. Silence somehow reminiscent of funerals and graveyards, reminder that prayers of repentance belong in the church! Reminds her of what she fears God might be. Therefore, Hope has spent most of her life avoiding both God and silence. Tonight she is less mindful because the quiet man near.

"This is the place where I live."

Hope points to a simple, but charming apartment building that occupies the street corner. It is no different from any of the dozen or so buildings they have passed, only this one distinctively her own.

"I live in the first apartment on the ground floor. I wouldn't live anywhere else because high places make me dizzy. --I suffer from so many fears! I hate myself for that. I guess you have no fear. Men like you are usually never afraid. It must be wonderful sometimes to be a man... to never be afraid..."

"Everyone has fear-- even men-- even a man like me battles fear at times. It is normal to be afraid in mortal presence. The fear of fear crawls into the mind, always prepared to pounce, always gnawing. Real fear is something else, something unexpected. Only after the flesh dies is there truly no more fear."

Hope shivers. She shivers because it is getting colder and because pitch of the wind now rising, which always causes her special alarm. Once inside she makes them tea while he kindles a fire. Not that it is necessary, since the apartment always maintained by thermostat control. However, a fire seems somehow more intimate, more reassuring.

The quiet man sits with his legs crossed upon a wooden rocking chair placed at edge of the fireplace cast in fluttering shadows, flames dancing within reflection of his flashing eyes.

Hope gives him a cup and spreads a sheepskin at the edge of the hearth. Next, she curls naturally upon the white fleece, preening like an animal, feels herself feline and predatory.

"Watch that you don't burn yourself," she whispers, desiring to capture him in her eyes, "the tea is very hot."

Hope says this with practiced sensuality cultivated through many years of experience. Only this night she means it more through less desire of this quiet man.

"Annick and I have lived here for three years. She's visiting with her father this weekend. He takes her whenever he can. He's a good man in that respect --very responsible. At least Annick will always have her father."

The quiet man says nothing back. A change has begun. Not change discernible to the moment. Rather a change emanating from a source deeper, as an areola of invisible hosts dances around his presence, like magnitude of distant stars, quivering through darkened atmosphere.

In one way, it frightens Hope. Another part of her feels inspired in both her body and imagination. She suddenly wishes that he would take her now! That his shadow would ascend naked over her like a marvellous fire god born this hour only to make Hope beautiful. Yet, this quiet man remains solitary in flickering light, which chisels new dimensions to already perfectly sculpted and disciplined cheekbones.

He must be part Russian, she decides, conceived through monarch lineage of Czars. Maybe his great grandfather one of those magnificent horsemen fabled to have power that tamed both horses and women of the north with only their eyes. She feels lost in eyes of this quiet man. Yes, Hope feels desire in his eyes, a desire so devouring that he refuses to violate pleasure of the moment.

He sees clearly the woman spread lovely as a sacrifice before his gaze. Her beauty made as a nearly transparent garment soon to slip away naked in time.

"You have nice hands," she remarks, pretending to trace his forearm and wrist with her red painted fingernail. "I knew a pianist whose hands were shaped like those of a woman. He played such lovely music... so lovely... so long ago..."

Hope's voice trails into shadow, her thoughts in the past constructed through memories of long ago.

"Your hands belong to a man. They say you can tell a lot about a man by studying his hands. First, you need to know what to look for. Your hands, for example, tell me that you are strong and sensitive. These are rare qualities to find on hands of one man."

"And what can be said about the hands of a woman?"

"Women are more difficult to read because they spend so much time and personal attention trying to cover up their hands. Yes, a woman is better able to conceal her mistakes."

"Then I guess that makes men more exposed-- more vulnerable to judgment."

"That is exactly the greatest difference between men and women! A man nearly always judges by what he sees, but for a woman life is more of a feeling than action that appears. A woman is accustomed to being vulnerable all the time. That's why we are forced to cover our imperfections. A man can't see the truth all at once because he's too quick to judge-- to reject anything flawed. It is better always to give a man illusion in the beginning. After that...maybe then he might accept something less perfect in his eyes."

"Is tonight an illusion?"

"It is difficult to say if I see through the heart or through something else. Perhaps I see a little both truth and illusion, mixed with hunger. Desire is like that, especially when a woman feels desire through eyes of a man."

"So are you saying that women have no true desire of their own?"

"Yes-- of course we do! Just somehow it is different for us. Our illusions come from within. I believe our dreams--

those of women-- more true! At least they are true in the beginning."

"Am I a dream in your mind?"

Hope is without reply. She has never met anyone like this quiet man. He seems capable somehow to penetrate into her thoughts. It bewitches her how he accomplishes this. How he can know so much in so short a time. It puzzles Hope why her deeper thoughts were to meet a man tonight. Puzzles her why she has invited this quiet man into the sanctuary of her heart and her home. There is something frightening about it all. Yes, he frightens her! Also, this quiet man excites Hope in a way not felt before!

"I just realize I do not know your name."

A blast of wind moans down the chimney and around corners of the building making the window shake in a way familiar to Hope. Flames in the fireplace spread flickering orange, while from a distance knells the faint sound of a bell. From her front window, Hope can see abandoned relic of the steeple etched into the skyline. As a child, Hope attended this church with her parents, attended weddings, and funerals, until one day her parents stopped loving. Eventually all the congregation moved away, leaving behind an empty shell. Like all the building in her neighbourhood it is old, representing obscure past of another generation better constructed, but less insulated compared to modern dwellings.

The quiet man turns, faces suddenly the window in anticipation to emptiness of her thoughts.

"There is mortality in the wind."

"What is the meaning of something like that? It just does that sometimes--only wind and nothing more!"

"Even wind has a beginning, a presence felt in the moment, and then passes on."

Hope feels herself suddenly cold inside.

"I don't like to think about death. There's more to life than dying. I saw my uncle on his deathbed waiting to die... later the funeral. I never want to see death again-- never!"

He only looks steadfast into her eyes. Hope feels a sense of apprehension beneath the calm of his gaze. She suddenly feels a new fear. Fear that he might change vicious-- become the true animal of his nature. Hope fears that maybe he knows more than he speaks, and that his words might purge the emptiness of her soul. But most she fears flames in the fireplace might altogether die, and only darkness between them.

Through sudden dread of this latest anxiety, she quickly decides to place another log on the fire. Excusing herself, Hope goes to the adjacent pantry separating the kitchen and fetches another piece of dry wood stacked near the gas stove. Upon returning, Hope unceremoniously drops the Birch log, causing embers to flutter around the rough stone fireplace.

"You are beauty!" She whispers, astonished by what she sees.

The quiet man has not moved from his place, only now he sits completely naked, with flesh as body of molten copper in reflecting shadow.

"I desire to see you as truly you are."

The tone of his voice commanding-- his eyes unwavering-- this quiet man knows what most she desires. And this night his desire is her desire.

"Why would you ask something like that of me? You have not even tried to kiss me--not even a familiar touch. And dare you ask me to strip naked for your pleasure?"

He says nothing, only continues to sit motionless, his expression calm. And snared within the depth of his eyes is silhouette of Hope as she sees herself, flames licking contour of a dissolving body with renewed hunger.

"I would tell you to leave, except... except..."

"There is no dishonour to be naked, to be exposed as you are. In time all the world must be as meant to be. Now is need for safety, need for warmth, and need for illusion. Now vanity made flesh so soon to perish. It is by design that all things change. All creation sealed in a scroll to end. Tonight fulfill measure of your name and shine in a heaven beyond this heaven as a star made new."

"I am too much shy. Come here and lie beside me on the hearth. Let us be warm together, touch each other in mystery, and be comforted by shared tenderness near the fire. It is, after all, better truth in present lie, than the lie of something that only might be true."

The quiet man remains frozen in time without moving, etched indelibly into the ink of surrounding darkness. Hope thinks his thoughts far away, and perhaps now he wants her less. She wishes him less demanding; wishes herself stronger. Yet, Hope's greatest anxiety is that he might altogether vanish, as so many other dreams in the past.

Hope turns her back to him, removes her blouse, and unfastens the hinge of her bra. She allows the polyester of her skirt to slip down her buttocks and fall inanimately onto the floor. She then peels slowly away the husk of her nylons, which she knows greater part of the illusion. After the last concealment drops away, Hope turns around, ashamed, her eyes looking down, concerned that the quiet man may be less pleased by what he sees.

The quiet man does not move, remains still in his place as a newly cast statue. Again changed in way Hope cannot describe. He says nothing, the muscles of his body tight and resisting; his eyes as suns fixed in a constellation devouring Hope completely in a way not known before. She wants desperately to touch the marble of his shoulders --wants his lips-- and to feel his strong unresisting hands press into the motion of her being.

"Beauty made time of fading illusion."

The sound of his voice touches her soul as something warm and pulsing, promising more than ever she could have imagined.

"Yes-- more than love-- greater than life!"

Hope begins to weep, her flesh consumed by singular vision of this moment. He is spirit of true beauty— more than being-- more than living! It is pain unbearable, a joy inconceivable. Hope filled, as never she has been full before. She feels her breast sensitive and satisfying. Her womb changed, suddenly capable of bearing love of the whole earth. Most of all Hope finds peace in universe of his vision— knows belonging through infinity in eyes of the quiet man.

"Please... please, come to me," she begs, as her own hands search the meaning of her body.

Her touch touches in absence of his touch, bringing her closer to his thoughts. It is release unfathomable-- an act of lust absolute!

"Please, be inside me that we might be one!"

But never does shadow of the quiet man descend over Hope. He does not frown or smile; nor judges the verity of this moment. He sits without moving, remaining timeless, and somehow apart, as the cries grow louder, continuing to rise like the rising of the wind outside. All the while Hope's flesh on fire-- all the while she is glad that he watches her!

Flames in the fireplace spread through agitation, casting embers of gold, reflecting sapphire shapes in nadir of surrounding darkness. Only now, he is changed completely light drawing ever nearer to the rhythm of her escalating ecstasy. Then expectantly sure the javelin of his soul rushes through Hope mortally as a force physical.

"Through blindness of vanity light changed darkness. Through shedding of illusion the soul released."

"Yes-- yes, I know-- God, now I know! --Yes, thank you-- so beautiful-- so beautiful!"

For the first time in life, Hope allows the sobs to flow from a keep locked secret deep within. She weeps because of all the fear of loneliness she has suffered always. She weeps for the husband she never loved, for the young horseman who taught her tenderness, and for Annick, who gives her courage to live from day to day.

Hope weeps because her mother and father no longer remember, and because her only sister now lives far away. Hope weeps most for the present, because the quiet man has come to set her mind and her body free at last.

"Sleep," his voice like the sound of silence pressed into silences. "Sleep, and dream the dream of this dream more perfect."

The quiet man seems now so far away, the heaviness lifted, as Hopes eyes begin to close against her will... irresistibly slow... forever.

Hope awakens because it is cold, because the fire only ashes now, and because brightness of morning light shines into her eyes. It is no longer snowing outside, the Quebec air fresh and pure. Beacon of the abandoned church steeple rises upon the horizon reflecting faithfully her memories. The abandoned symbol of abiding hope contrasted against a world of material excess, no longer recognizing its true value.

Yes, Hope likes her country-- likes divergence of the seasons and freshness in the air. It is something to see even on Saint Valentine's Day. The quiet man is gone. Only Hope knows with certainty if ever he was real.

5

Eclipse

*A*lice Be is not even tired by the time she reaches the rocky mountain pass leading from Vail. She left Los Angeles city limits on Thursday evening heading out into no man's land. Had spent fourteen hours nonstop in Las Vegas, where she met a high-roller with another kind of suffering, who claimed not to care as long as the dice hot in one hand and a cold drink in the other. Now it is long past sunset, and Alice knows she ought to rest. She has driven all night and all day through parts of the Mojave to Utah's Bad Lands, then crossing over onto the Colorado Plateau. Outside Grand Junction Alice stopped to eat a tasteless meal, washed-down by four cups of coffee. That was nearly three hours ago, and she should be exhausted by now. But there is no rest for Alice Be, no escaping the

Furies of anger and confusion that have tormented her thoughts mile after desert mile.

"Where you headed?" The gas attendant enquires in a husky voice used to the cold.

"Denver."

"Denver," he repeats, gazing apprehensively up into the blackness of the sky. "You got yourself family there?"

"My father once lived there. I've never been to Denver. It sounds like some place lost in the clouds. Father thought that too, when he moved there after divorcing mother."

"Looks to me like a bad storm a-coming. If you take my advice you'll bed down somewhere near here for the night. These passes can be damned tricky even on a clear sunny day. But you try and drive them when there's ice and snow it's like the very devil come into these mountains!"

Alice knows this to be good advice. Given the weather, Denver is at least two, maybe three hours ahead, and she sees in this man's eyes that his intentions good. But the rage will not allow her to listen to better reason. So Alice Be pays for the gas, saying only that she will think about it.

Although she smiles, within seethes anger she cannot even define. Not against anything present, not against anyone particular, it is just raw fury bred of selfishness by others, and general injustice of the world as it is. Always the rage near, just below the surface, at times clear and present. Anger aimed against her father for abandoning Alice's mother after twenty six years of marriage and escaping into the Western Rockies. Anger turned inward that compels Alice six months later to marry out of spite a man she did not even love and move to Georgia. A man who took her night after night for nearly two years, as if he were man-handling a sack of coffee at his warehouse job. The doctor called her infertile, but Alice knew the real reason. She knew it the rage that prevented anything from being conceived. Then, finally he signed all the divorce papers, glad to be rid of her. So she quits the teaching position at a public junior high school she had taken just for the money, a position suited for a married woman living in the Atlanta suburbs. After the divorce the job and the salary prove no longer compatible. But still the rage remains.

So she packed her few belongings into the trunk of her car and headed west, stopping in New Orleans, and then into Texas crossing the Panhandle. From here she picks-up the fabled Route 66 into California, all the way to the Pacific.

Southern California would be a new beginning. They call this the *City of Lost Angels*, a place in the sun that never sleeps. A place where she can forget and be anyone she wants to be. Alice becomes mesmerized by the lights and the glitter of a city that promises everything and takes everything. In time, Alice realizes this to be the belly of purgatory, with a pulse always beating, always moving, but never truly alive. For seven years she lives as a seraph, fluttering from alley to alley, giving everything, but receiving so little in return. And the rage only grows stronger still, changing worse than before.

She cannot even count days and nights that flicker by without her even noticing, as always another illusion appears just within her grasp. During those seven years, she reached optimistically toward the stars; every year remembered the same looking back at them now. Faces that come and go, blending into a changing tapestry of light and shadow--Alice's own face no longer she recognizes. A face etched with fine lines made dry by days spent baking under the California sun. Her visage changed, reflecting betrayal and pain of emptiness, which seeps from the slits of her green eyes. In the anonym of this hidden principality on the edge of night, Alice turns to alcohol and drugs, runs a gauntlet of late parties and treks of passing adventure in an attempt to burn away the poison in her veins. Then one morning before sunrise, she awakens in a park under the stars, wondering how she got there. This is when she makes the decision to change everything. But mostly Alice determines once and for all to rewrite the past.

"You have the eyes of your aunt--*beautiful sorceress eyes!*" Her father often reminded her when growing up. "This is why your mother and I named you Elyssa in honor to my twin sister."

Alice never knew this aunt, because she died in an automobile accident before Alice born. Nevertheless, she is branded for all life with both eyes and name of a stranger that only brings tears to her father's eyes. Why that name? For so many years the name Elyssa became a brand of inescapable tragedy. Not her sadness, but the sadness of her father, who refused to let go of the ghost in his mind. So he named his only daughter Elyssa, as an epitaph of memorial too great for her to bear.

The last name of her father is Bernard; her married name Banner. She wants to use neither name. So this moment Alice decides it is the right time to change everything. Her father would not like it, but at least her mother understood. The following week she makes an appointment with the court of public records for application of a legal name change and is re-born Alice Be. No long just Elyssa--no longer that girl from the past with pretty green eyes! No longer will she remain the sad shadow in her father's eyes because of a lost sibling. Through this act of rebellion, Alice erases the past, arising from ashes as a phoenix stamped with a new name and new beginning. It is the name of her choosing, decisively and legally her own!

The windshield wipers labor tediously against the accumulating barrage. The night is cold. Not as cold as it might have been, because hint of snow had been in the early forecast. Drone of the engine changes to silence, a silence so deep that Alice has no desire to disturb it. At least this lack of any true noise helps her to escape the bedlam of voices that invade her thoughts continually. At least consistency of a sound, not sound, creates a peace within. Yes, just now she appreciates the constant artificial hush, especially because it is a quiet not true quiet. Usually, Alice did not like to be alone with only her own thoughts. Perhaps, she even fears the deeper truth of real solitude. Because all adds up to the grave in the end--fear of death being the greatest of all fears! Now Alice accepts inevitability as being the only sure course, choosing in the moment present to banish all logic of discourse from her mind, preferring the constant hum of the car engine to navigate course of inevitability she is powerless to change.

The miles stretch tediously ahead, vanishing into the oblivion of the rearview mirror. Humped eclipses of the great continental mountains divide shadows from shadows, sliced through by a ribbon of headlights. She feels their presence only, the strong shoulders of these sublime giants huddled beneath centuries that altogether dwarf the shade of her brief existence within context of vast topography. They stand collectively as footstools to a greater earth, most of which Alice has never seen and probably will never see. The heavens silent witness stretched into a void dividing night and day. It squashes her imagination to consider distances between each star on a clear night, or the time it takes light to cross from there to here. The beginning of creation only glimpsed through mortal comprehension. Then what? It seems that the heaven and earth once she knew, only a fabled memory of someone else. And only Alice Be remains in this empty corner of the universe.

A month after reinventing herself, Alice meets Sam, a friend she can count on. A friend who only wants the best for everyone--not a user--not like the creature Elyssa had become. Sam different from all the rest--special in a way that makes Alice sometimes uncomfortable--unlike anyone she has ever known. Someone capable of seeing farther than most people wish to imagine-- to look deeper than many dare. Alice felt frightened in the beginning, frightened because of the emotions awakened. Alice denies she could ever feel that way--denies that passion still remained smoldering in a heart she was sure dead. Only now she feels trapped in another kind of guilt. A web from which there seems no escape. In desperate attempt she makes impulsive decision to leave Sam and Los Angeles to return east and live with her mother for fear of altogether losing herself. But Sam is too wise, too much connected to the deeper meanings of things, has experienced rejection before and knows what Alice really means.

"You cannot keep running always from the truth," Sam says, cornering her. "Sooner or later you must face who you really are."

"I know who I am not--and the person I am today needs something more! Something I have not yet found! Maybe it is something no one has to give, but I must continue to try. You are a good person and I care about you Sam, but not in the same way."

"I know," Sam solemnly replies with glassy eyes that say even more. "At least call me once by my real name. I am Samantha and I love you."

"I am sorry that I cannot be what you want me to be."

In the end it is Sam that leaves, quietly, and without malice. At least this kind of abandonment familiar--at least this emotion Alice Be can control. Then a week later, Alice receives phone call from her mother that father has died. The funeral scheduled in Denver, where they will meet to perform the final arrangements.

In this moment of deep reflection, Alice Be forgets where she is--forgets the sharpness of the curves, the narrow passage in front nearly erased by foaming blizzard of cascading ice. With only darkness forged in an oblivious clouded lens of the rearview mirror. Then slow motion of events, time suspended in a stream forever now.

Cars in opposite lanes swerve just in time. It is so automatic that it seems someone else at the wheel, Alice watching the event remotely. The other vehicle recedes into darkness, lights flashing wildly, horn blasting like a fire messenger sent to prevent Alice from reaching any further into a strait forbidden.

Momentarily shaken, Alice Be concentrates, focusing on the white ribbon of the parting passage in front of her. She inserts a recorded tape by Bonnie Tyler, playing and replaying the haunting lyrics of a song named "*Total Eclipse of the Heart*". This is her song now. It resounds as statement everlasting in a world of changing faces and confusing memories. She starts singing along, shouting insanely the refrain "*Total Eclipse of the Heart!*" In this moment Alice Be poised at a precipice dividing the present. The past a scribbled diary written in black ink upon parchment of shadows; the future a place not yet inscribed; and Alice Be recorded somewhere in the middle.

It begins snowing more heavily, white petals of luminescence changing into a barrage of snowball clumps smashing defiantly against the windshield, reminder that the world beyond never truly predictable, never really safe.

Suddenly, a sign blazes to her attention. At first she thinks the letters figment of imagination. Slowing down, she reads carefully *Alice Be Exit in 3 Miles*. She bites her tongue to be sure she is still awake and not dreaming. Whatever this is, it is not a dream! Alice had studied carefully the roadmap before entering these mountains. Surely she would not have missed the coincidence of a place bearing her new name.

The miles on the speedometer click apprehensively away, until finally a second sign appears. It reads *Alice Be This Exit*. Without further deliberation, Alice finds herself on the exit road. She reasons because she is tired, because the storm more severe now. But deep down Alice knows that neither these facts the true reason. It is a place with her name, a place curious and somehow frightening. Coincidence or consequence, Alice Be hears calling of her name from within twisted passage of these Colorado mountains. A voice she cannot ignore.

The road unpaved and poorly defined. It inclines sharply, a thick layer of snow and ice creating an obstacle course with dangerous slick spots. Alice thinks to turn back, only there are no turn-offs, the passage narrow, gutted on both sides. Just when she decides to chance the maneuver anyway, Alice Be arrives at her destination.

It is altogether bizarre, charmingly familiar, and hauntingly surreal. The hotel resort still retains monarch dignity, just as she remembers. The European elegance of baroque architecture unmistakable, transporting Alice back in time.

She might have been so very young then, filled with dreams and excitation of many possibilities. A trip through Europe, a desire ever since she was a little girl read stories by her father from a book named Grimm's Fairy Tales each night before falling to sleep. These stories of whimsical characters elevate her young imagination in belief of things supernatural.   But it is in the Black Forest region of Germany that most inspires apprehension that there is more truth than fantasy to these tales.

It is while visiting the Alsatian French city of Strasbourg that she meets a local divorced archeology professor conducting a field trip with a group of students. He speaks such charming English, convincing her to accompany them on a day's hike into the pleasant Vosges Mountains to see some of the older castles that still remain in the region. She easily accepts, and later they go out for dinner at a Moroccan restaurant he knows located in Kehl, a small border town on the German side of the Rhine. She thinks of him as she might her father while growing up. Turns out he wants her as a man that hungers for companionship of a woman. After an uncomfortable exchange a negotiated compromise reached. Alice determines this the last time she allows a man to buy her dinner. Before parting company she asks him if the Black Forest Mountain on the German side of the Rhine River the same as Vosges.

"You might call them estranged sisters," the man says, his eyes smiling wily. "Both run along the Rhine, but never really meet. There is a bus you can take that leaves early in the morning. In less than a day of travel and you are at the town of Baden-Wurttemberg, Germany. I think you would find the excursion rewarding by what you have shared with me about your bedtime stories. The Black Forest is like none other."

Alice thanks the man, whose kindness she considers tainted by his desire. She arrives in Baden-Wurttemberg the next afternoon. Her attempts to find a guide prove futile, since no one brave enough to enter the forest on the night they call "Hexennacht" or the Witches Night. Because Alice has only one more week before her flight back to America departing Berlin, she decides to go alone.

The following morning she begins to hike along the well defined trails of the Schwarzwald Mountains. It is everything her child's mind imagined. Hosts of monarch trees stand as strong regiments, the massive limbs of their arms spreading into a jungle fuse. Beneath their shadows are moss-covered boulders with giant mushrooms sprouting between blackened crevices bleeding through veins of limestone. If only her father were here to see. A little past noon Alice stops to refresh herself at the base of a large Birch tree with an issue of fresh water flowing through maze of exposed roots. Here she finds a most unusual white flower, the petals shot through with dark red veins. Plucking the prize, Alice places it near to her heart.

"It is rare to find such a flower in these woods." A voice speaks behind her.

Startled, Alice turns to face the most unique person of anyone she has ever met. It is not so much the appearance only, but the androgynous presence of this individual, almost mythical. The legs shaven smooth as her own, a body strong like chiseled granite, common to Germanic people of the mountains, long blond hair and beautiful azure eyes.

"You are the first person I have encountered since early this morning."

"Yes, I come here often. My family has lived in this region even before Germany became a Country. Judging by your accent you are American?"

"Yes, I came to Europe for vacation. I just finished university and wanted to see the world before deciding to settle down."

"You Americans are always thinking about settling down somewhere. Here always we are home. I suppose this is the greatest difference between our continents. My name is Kristen. Perhaps we can share the trail together?"

"You can call me Alice."

The young girl feels immediately at ease by the calm of this person, but chooses nevertheless to remain secretive. Alice was her secret name even then, a name she shared rarely with a few, a name of protection and of her own choosing. They begin talking and laughing as though they had known each other always. Being local to the region, Kristen knows much about the Black Forest. Knows more than Alice thinks.

"This forest is backbone to the earth," Kristen says with spread arms. "Kings and Warlords have fought and perished among these trees. Nowhere is blood more rich than in the Black Forest. Since beginning it is named the enchanted wood, a place where dreams and fears entangle to reach into the world beyond. It is said that one must be careful of thoughts here; otherwise the spirit trapped within the wood might hear."

"It all sounds fantastically dreadful!" Alice says charmed.

"My mother also recited to me stories when I was a child. She said that a long time ago, before the Hapsburgs, even before Prussia a kingdom, a time when German people were pure in innocence, this forest was like any other on the face of the earth. Then there wandered into it a dispossessed sorcerer wounded and close to death. Not desiring that his enemies overwhelm him as he slept, the sorcerer conjures legions of spirits for protection. But he died before morning light, leaving those spirits trapped within these trees. Since that time, the Black Forest has remained a place steeped in dark mysticism, dangerous to the unguarded imagination of all that might seek refuge in the shade of these trees. Of course my mother was superstitious about most things, so for her this story true."

"Do you believe there is any truth to the story?"

Alice desires to penetrate to the heart of the conversation, to see the world through Kristen's eyes, to feel in this forest as only a local born from this earth might feel.

"I believe that whatever is fashioned from this wood by thought or by deed possessed with life and power its own. A reflection only, but of substance no less real, this is soul of this place: a place remaining invisible to the light of men."

They talk about other things; things that make no sense and things meaningful only to the fancy of a young girl. As the sun begins to set and shadows grow longer, Kristen claims to know a place nearby where they might camp for the night. At cleft of twilight they arrive at the askew gates of a decaying edifice. This once elegant estate now snared in a web of twisting foliage, the home abandoned since many years. Here they will make a fire near the skeleton of a dry fountain.

Almost she has forgotten that night; almost it has changed into a dream, only some of it still lucid in her mind. Now she finds herself transfixed in this present, seeing through eyes of another dream no less, yet no more real.

The facade of this present architecture so exact that almost Alice believes it could have been moved stone by stone and resurrected here. Lights shine inviting through opaque windows, sure sign of the living, in contrast to that other place dead in the past. Alice imagines well dressed men and women dancing to melodic tune of another century. How she wishes to join them and glide freely light as air. This part of fantasy she will keep reserved to the dreams of a younger girl.

There are no other cars in the area, which Alice thinks odd. Had she not been tired, perhaps she would have pondered this more. Parking her vehicle in a convenient spot near the porch entrance, Alice determines to go inside. Surely there will be a vacancy, since it obvious no one else so foolish as to be on these precarious mountain roads this particular night of a storm.   If not, then she would remain in the lobby until worst of the storm passed.

Alice is about to close the door when she realized that the headlights still on. As she reaches inside to turn the switch, something else catches her attention which amazes her even more. In front appears a white sign printed in large red letters that reads *Reserved for Alice Be.*

Alice shivers. A bizarre feeling of *déjà vu* creeps from within another forgotten corner of her mind, a feeling of someplace she has never left. Nor is it the first time she feels this way, She decides that as coincidental as it may seem, there must surely be another Alice Be.

Mask of Her Reflection in Venus

Alice slams shut the car door, pushing that memory down into the recess of a past only vaguely familiar. Inside it is exactly what she always imagined a place like this would be. Ornate furnishings embellish a grand lobby with marble floors and intricately carved archways that rise monolithic toward high ceilings with a crystal chandelier suspended in the center. Near the entrance is an oak front desk absent of a clerk. Alice thinks the sound of music in her mind only, a haunting tune mixed with several familiar intonations. It grows now more perceptible, coming from behind two curtained glass-pane doors to her left etched by light reflected from within. Part of her wants to open the barricade and pass through to the other side, part of her content to remain without. Turning again to face the counter, her eyes meet those of an officious presence peering steadfastly through lens of horn-rimmed glasses with an expression void of emotion.

"I'm sorry," Alice flusters. "The music so strange, yet lovely; it is like nothing I have ever heard before."

"Music...there is no music."

"Just before you came back I swear I heard music playing in the next room behind those closed doors."

"Before I came back from where? I have always been here. Where else would I be?"

Alice did not particularly like the arrogant tone that so reminds her of a waiter in Paris, who smirked openly because of her "*quaint colonial*" accent. This hotel clerk cut from the same cloth, with globular eyes dark as perdition, like those of a cemetery rodent surviving on scraps from the living.

"Never mind, but I am sure I heard music coming from in there," she says, pointing to the doors.

"The banquet room has remained unoccupied for as long as I have been here. I am sure you are mistaken."

There is that annoying tone of arrogant superiority again. Alice defiantly walks over and attempts to open the doors. They are most assuredly locked, only darkness within, only silence, and only Alice Be certain it not just her imagination.

"Allow me to check your reservation," the clerk says with detached stoicism, opens a large book on the counter, and begins scrolling his slender fingers down the registry entries, his eyes darting beadily back and forth.

"Oh, I have no reservation--"

"Yes--here it is. Reservation for party of one under the name Alice Be from Los Angeles. Your room is number 36, top of the stairs, third door on the left."

"It's not possible," Alice insists, demanding to see the entry.

There appears the name Alice Be in clear letters along with today's date. It perplexes her how this could be. Before tonight she knew nothing of this place, or even that she might find herself chased by a storm into maze of these mountain passages. Nothing about any of this makes sense.

Alice might have left then, only the wind outside has increased in ferocity, howling around the eaves of the roof, making the windows and doors shudder. What did it matter anyway? Here she has promise of a room and warm bed for the night. The rest she would sort out tomorrow.

The shiny skeleton key slips snuggly into the lock of room number 36 and turns easily. The chamber, sparsely furnished, is as quaint as any she might have wished for. A double bed dominates center of the room with satin pillows and a matching bedspread embroidered with pastoral scenery depicting a typical German theme. The handcrafted umbrella of a tiffany lamp sits atop a simple night table made of mahogany with a glossy mirror finish that reflects darkly her visage. For some reason that she does not wish to fathom, what she sees disturbs her, and Alice quickly looks away, preferring not to gaze too deeply.

The washroom is little more than a closet equipped with a basin, a large pitcher of water, and a dry toilet centered round an aperture. It may not be a luxury suite, but will most certainly do for the night.

It is the very absence of luxury that reminds Alice suddenly of her grandfather. She was only twelve when he went away, and always he represents in her mind a Merlin of flowers capable of extraordinary magic. He lived alone on a farm outside of Athens, a kind and gentle soul having ability to communicate with animals as though they were people.

Every second weekend after death of his mother, Alice's father insisted on packing the family station wagon to make the two and a half hour drive from New York to visit his father. Mother never cared much for the journey, but endured with only a few sighs of complaint.

"Papa, you ought to sell this place and come live with us," she remembers her father saying often to grandfather.

"No, I don't think I could ever do that. This land is like my own flesh. All my memories are here, your mother, you just a boy growing up. Everything I got worth living for is here on this farm. Anywhere else I am just an old man, but here, I am keeper of many things."

"But, Papa, what if something happens and you need a doctor?"

"Someday, son, you will understand. I am well in myself. Here I have purpose and am happy. Ask yourself: Could you give those things to an old man living in your home? We each have our own path of responsibilities. God just made it that way. And nobody and nothing is meant to remain here forever. Time is short in this old world, and to spend too much time worrying about tomorrow only robs us of the precious time we got left."

Perhaps it was this simple philosophy that added so much charm to his presence. In her young mind he seemed to make time for everything, from fixing his tractor or mending chicken wire, to sunning with his granddaughter in a field richly laced with green clovers. The clouds above his farm different somehow, shapes transformed wondrously by command of his deep baritone voice capable of transporting his young Elyssa to grand castles of imagination existing in celestial streams. There she saw fairy princesses and gallant knights with thistle swords and acorn shields. Closer to earth she is introduced to giant dragonfly monsters, hording warrior ants, and silly blundering June Bugs--all endowed with unique personalities through mimicry of her grandfather's masterful storytelling. Most terrifying of all, the praying mantis, which mercilessly rips its victims apart! The ugly and the beautiful, the vicious and the harmless, coexisting in a world where a man's footprint becomes a dangerous valley and a discarded paper roll a tunnel of love. But he also shares with her other things, things that no one else knew about. Like the star children, who sometime fall out of the sky at night and seem to be born as any other child, except that they have powers, which appear magic to all except the innocent of this world. It is through them that good survives even in places dark and evil. He opens her imagination to existence of secret of moon-drop castles built each night by fireflies, and are inhabited from twilight to twilight, only to change into dust by morning. But if someone old were fortunate enough to find the dust of such a castle, then immediately that person would transform back into innocence and begin all over again. He was truly wondrous in her eyes, a magician extraordinaire, who plucked lilacs out of the air and planted them in his granddaughter's auburn hair.

"Grandfather, are you going to die one day?"

"Why do you ask such a thing?"

"Because father says he is afraid you will die out here all alone."

"That is because your father has such little faith."

"But grandmother died...and you and her are about the same age."

"Child nothing in this world is alive or is dead." He says, his gruff hand engulfing that of the little girl. "Each spring you see return of the same birds from the sky, the same flowers blossom into light, and the same bees taking their honey. Through every passage caterpillars shrivel within cocoon tombs, only to awaken as butterflies reborn. All things live in the mind of God, who thought all things into existence, gives bounty to every season, and is definition of everlasting. God did not make things to die, but to live forever."

"Then where is grandmother now?"

"My wonderful Camellia rides winds of the stars, circling rim of the universe, and is now and forever part of everything that has ever been or will ever be."

"Is she an angel now?"

"No child, she is more than an angel, more than all the elements. She is at threshold of the beginning waiting for all that must follow. This is what your father does not yet understand, but in time his mind will awake."

Then one Sunday after Easter, they travel to see her grandfather, but not at his farm. They go instead to a large white house with a circular driveway surrounding a wide green lawn. There were several parked cars, with clusters of people outside. Some Elyssa knows as relatives, most all the others complete strangers. The white oblong parlor hurt her eyes at first, the morning sun streaming brightly through host of windows facing east.

"Elyssa come we must say goodbye to grandpapa," her father solemnly says with tears in his eyes; then takes her hand and steps toward a polished black coffin at one end of the chamber with a reposed life-like manikin inside.

"Why, where is he going?" She demands shyly, dragging her steps.

Her mother holds tightly to her other hand, not saying anything.

"He is gone to be with Jesus in heaven, Elyssa."

"Oh, just that," She sighs with relief. "I thought he was going somewhere terrible. Now he can ride the wind with Grandmother free at last."

Her parents just look at their daughter without saying a word.

Yes, her grandfather would approve the meagerness of these accommodations. Not just approve, but embrace it more as an adventure than inconvenience of comfort. Compared to the rustic simplicity of his farm, this hotel estate is a royal principality. She doubts, however, that he would consider it a home large enough to accommodate his many friends born of imagination.

Alice feels suddenly the intensity of these past few days weigh upon her. Changing into a cotton flannel nightgown retrieved from her night bag, she closes the lamp and slips exhausted beneath the covers. Tonight Alice Be would rest in comfort. Tomorrow will be time enough to sort out these many perplexities.

Alice dreams-- or at least she believes she is dreaming. It is night, and she is back again in the Black Forest of Germany with Kristen. The abandoned estate squats as a dark shadow engulfing the lighter shades of surrounding gloom. No lunar presence dominates the sky of this night, the stars distant and enigmatic imprinted on a black shroud, with only the kindled flames of a flickering fire provoking semblance of light.

"Why would no one from the village hike into the forest on this day?" Alice enquires.

"Superstition, perhaps fear of darkness, but mostly ignorance keeps them in the illusion of security. Tonight is beginning of a New Moon, when face of darkness prevails.

Mask of Her Reflection in Venus

Truth is they are never really safe... even though they hide beyond the fortress of this forest. This is a lesson yet to be learned. Such a night as this reminds them of what most they fear. It is reminder of shadows lurking in shades of their own darkness, and how little of themselves they truly know...until the last embers bleed away and there is no light at all."

Alice feels suddenly apprehensive. Why would her new friend be speaking this way? The red shards of their campfire glow excitedly, reflecting the depth of Kristen's soul sending chills through her body.

"I begin to understand why this is called the Black Forest. It seems I am still a little girl hiding under my blanket as father read from pages of fairy tale. Particularly frightening was the story about a boy named Hansel and girl named Gretel. But most I remember the evil witch! I know that for me to think about a children's bedtime story after so many years must sound silly to you.   But... just now the story so clear in my mind."

"Many stories have been told about this place--many lost in these woods never to return."

"Any stories that you know are true?" Alice enquires.

"There is one in particular...but to many his is the tale of a villain."

"I like to hear about villains. They are the ones that makes stories most interesting."

Kristen gazes deeply into the night with vision that sees more than the darkness only.

"A Baron once lived in this mansion. One that loved too much...and not enough! This Baron was a man of complex character believing that magic--even dark magic-- might be used for good."

"Was this long ago?"

"Only a few know for certain how long. The Baron was a proud monarch, heir to an ancient royal family going back of the Austro-Hungarian Empire. This before

Germany joined forces with Austria during the First World War. This Baron became estranged from the world outside his mansion, isolating himself and his sickly wife from politics of change. Some say he went mad, sacrificing his beloved to the spirit of these woods and ritualistically drinking her blood."

"That's absolutely dreadful!"

"To those outside it might appear that way, but for the Baron it meant chance of salvation."

"How can something so monstrous be considered salvation?"

"He was a man left with few choices. His wife was dying, the monarchy failing, and now aware his principality perished already. In desperation the Baron turned to the dark arts, appealing to the magic of these woods, thus making the ultimate sacrifice. Do not think it an easy decision. Things in the past are not always simply explained in the present. But do not worry, it is only another legend."

"So in the end what happened to this Baron?"

"Some say that because of his cruel decision he became cursed to live forever in the bark of this forest. To those born in this region, the Black Forest is not a place only, but a domain of spiritual incursion. On each anniversary of Walpurgisnacht, the Baron takes on mortal appearance to try and warn those inexperienced in ways of real magic. It is even commonly reported that Germany's Fuhrer once came to these woods to know if the legends of the Baron true. They say that here is where he saw vision of his cruel destiny."

"You mean Adolf Hitler came here!"

"Many souls remain trapped here. There are those that came before and many others since--all lost in confusion of this dark forest. Only some that might escape; but none by power of their own will. In course you will know and you will be. It is within you to decide."

Mask of Her Reflection in Venus

Alice awakens. This is not the conversation she remembers having. Now that past vague in her mind--so much about the true world escapes her in this present. She rouses out of bed and turns on the light. Looking again into depth of the polished wood of the night table she again sees in the dark wood her own reflection. In the background is someone else, with eyes almost familiar. Startled she spins around, but no one there! The bed empty, nor is there anyone else in the room. Quickly changing out of her nightgown and repacking her bag, Alice determines to leave this place. She decides even a storm in the Rocky Mountains a choice more favorable than this haunted hotel.

The check-in desk is deserted, as when first she arrived, which she thinks little surprising. Upon opening the front entrance, Alice is met by a nearly impassable barrier of snow reaching half way up the doorpost, her vehicle completely interred in a drift. But this not the only reason she is condemned to remain. Dangling in the ignition of the locked car is her only set of keys. Nor is it the first time this mistake made. Returning inside, Alice again hears music coming from inside the banquet room. Upon approach she sees through cracks of light shadows moving within. Still the double doors refuse to yield to her pressure. Whipping around she is certain someone behind her, but no one there.

"I wish to have service!" She shouts. "This is Alice Be in room 36."

The music stops; the cracks of light fade into darkness. Only Alice Be remains alone, trapped in the belly of this hotel bearing her name.

Alice laughs because of the irony of her situation, because her shoes and clothing unsuited for the elements outside. She laughs at her own foolishness, and the impulsiveness of her nature to take an exit just because it bore the vanity of her name. Mostly she laughs because this not the first time pride of her vanity has directed Alice along a path of deception--something that happened not so very long ago.

Alice had told Sam that she wanted to go to the theatre alone. At least this was in part the truth. In reality she wanted something more, something absent in the present. It all began months earlier after joining a correspondence group with mandate to choose a name from list of complete strangers and write a letter. Her choice is someone using a Post Office Box in the San Fernando Valley. In like fashion, Alice also engages service of the U. S. Post Office as her return address. Just the idea of anonymity provides Alice a sense of invisibility that excites her imagination, making her feel somehow powerful and in control.
Her choice is Oscar Simon, a name odd in her mind evoking curiosity. When this Oscar Simon responds a week later, Alice feels boosted in her ego. The correspondence is mundane in the beginning, mostly about living in California from aspect of their perspective location. It becomes clear by the third letter that Oscar Simon not a superficial person, but one serious in contemplation, with each letter becoming more distinguished in her thoughts. This exchange went on for weeks, each letter more confiding, more intimate. Finally, Alice determines she must meet Oscar Simon face to face. But to her surprise and disappointment, she receives a very polite, but definite decline.
"My dear friend Alice Be, I am flattered --no more than flattered-- I am enamored by your desire that we meet. Unfortunately, this is impossible at the present. I am an actor and a playwright, presently in the heat of a very important project. I know that you must understand when I say that my time is limited even to the exclusion of the

more fragrant moments in life. Nevertheless, I reserve the hope that at some future date we may bare our souls and see truth truthfully blind to imperfection."

An actor and a playwright! Alice wonders what kind of material he wrote. Surely they would be romantic, and with much adventure. His words continue to incubate inside her curiosity week after week, sometimes as many as three in a row. This Oscar Simon intrigues her more than anyone she has ever known. He is perfect in Alice's imagination, a hero without comparison, making anyone else flawed and mortal. Often she catches herself reciting to friends-- even sometimes to Sam--something he stated in one of his letters, as though it were an excerpt from a manifesto of better instruction. Then unexpectedly an invitation arrives at her door by special courier.

It reads: "You are humbly invited to the opening debut of Oscar Simon's play titled: The Toy Menagerie" behind the Chinese Theatre near Hollywood and Vine."

Below is the exact address, date, and time. Of the list of performers, only Oscar Simon is familiar. And for this singular reason Alice Be will go to the debut. No longer will he remain an enigma in her mind. At last she would see him in the flesh! But the nagging unanswered question in her mind: How could he possibly know her home address?

Nevertheless, this special invitation surpasses even her most guarded fantasies. Alice often imagined a happenstance of bumping into him at a Mall or while running on the beach at sunset. She would know him through intensity of his eyes, and he would immediately know her. But to meet him for the first time during moment of greatest achievement--to be in some way part of his success--to share even a little this hour of fame-- represents an occasion indeed!

The day of the play, Alice goes shopping for a new dress and new shoes. Has her hair and nails done by a professional (which was something she rarely did), even goes so far as to have an arrangement of white roses delivered at end of the performance.

The lights dim, the curtains part--the play begins. Silhouettes appear against the backdrop, tall men with sharp handsome features, and equally endowed women. Then a voice, strong, clearly masculine, soothingly addresses the audience.

"My name is Oscar Simon. I have conceived and composed this play out of the inspiration of life's many stages and for your edification as my audience. The actors you are about to see are real, the scenes illusion of events designed to force believability. The world is indeed a script, and all of us unwilling characters cast to play parts to the last scene. The Toy Menagerie is a play that represents moment of pause, an intermission from roles enacted since beginning, a synoptic break in reality, where all things possible, and yet nothing as it truly is. In the story about to unfold mice excel to the glory of men, and men reduced to something less than the polished vision of collective pride. In this constructed menagerie all equal in measure, limited only by personal prejudice and reason. So let this play of imagination and foolish dreams begin!"

The stage lights brighten slowly, with the silhouettes diminishing in size, growing smaller and smaller, until one realizes that they are only shadows of dolls poised atop a small table. Beside the table is a swivel arm chair, back facing the audience.

"You have seen the shadows of dolls and were filled with expectation to see their image," the voice of Oscar Simon continues. "Now behold yet another shape, another transformation, yet to be transformed."

The chair swivels suddenly around. Awe and silence sweeps through the crowd. Sitting in the chair is a man with striking handsome face, wearing a neatly trimmed beard, and with clear blue intelligent eyes. But Oscar

Mask of Her Reflection in Venus

Simon is like no man Alice has ever seen. His body misshapen, he reminds her of a broken doll. Rising from the chair with the aid of a cane, it becomes immediately clear that Oscar Simon is a humpbacked dwarf, less than five feet tall.

Four actors parade on stage, all born with obvious handicaps, each as charismatic as Oscar Simon. There is a woman on crutches dressed like Raggedy Anne balancing on wooden legs. A second woman bound to a wheelchair with withered right arm, a watermelon head, and whose appendages dangle useless as uncontrollable tentacles. In tow behind the wheelchair a small wagon with a man's body perched robustly in the center having neither arms nor legs. Perhaps the most disturbing is a particularly articulate young man, who came into this world featureless, without eyes, and completely hairless.

The scenes that follow are remarkable. From the moment the play begins, the audience forgets the handicaps of these actors. Oscar Simon arises suddenly and miraculously as a giant. He is no longer that dwarf of a man. He is now a stage prodigy superimposed upon the imagination of all caught in his magic. In defiance to the anger of her disappointment, even Alice is swept away in awe. This is the man she knew by letters--not that silly looking dwarf! This is the man she so dreamed to meet one day! Then a voice inside her head reminds her of the deception--Oscar Simon and the dwarf one and the same! He should have told her! Why this trick of nature?

Alice begins to suffocate. Illusion and reality fade in and out of her mind, until finally she must escape. Even before the first act finished, Alice slips discreetly from the VIP section and rushes out of the theater. She remains parked in a nearby alley seated in her car smoking cigarette after cigarette, paralyzed, unwilling even to think.

She continues to sit even after the audience spews into the street during intermission. Discreetly she watches from a distance as some talk, others smoke making faces of ridicule, and still others that choose this opportunity to slip quietly away. The dedicated turn back for the second part of the entertainment, and still Alice refuses to move from her position, intentionally remaining obscure like a spy without. Why had she reacted this way? Is the source of her rage because Oscar Simon handicapped or because he had not disclosed his condition to her? Did this make him less of a man, or only less to the standard of her imagination? Still--he had no right to lead her on that way! For reasons she could not understand, Alice feels betrayed. But betrayed by who or what? Oscar Simon was not born by choice, as were none of the other actors in this gruesome play! Why had Oscar Simon written such a thing? This Toy Menagerie was nothing more than a slap against the roulette of nature--a poke into the eye of God! How dare this Oscar Simon to be so presumptuous as to judge society by measure of imperfect standard. Mostly, Alice feels confused, feels utterly wicked, and at the same time ashamed and abandoned. Yes, this was it! She feels abandoned by God! Why would a benevolent God allow so cruel of a sentence upon humanity? Oscar Simon was the noblest person she had ever communicated with, but turns out to be a deformed dwarf! Yes, the joke is on her! It especially angers her that he invited her to this outrageous play. Wishes he had just left her with the fantasy of her own conception. Then Alice realizes the short coming not his, but a measure against the darker nature of expectation--the judgment her own! This ugly truth she would have to live with for the rest of life.

The theater now dark, the street vacant, and only Alice Be remains in the solitude of her own making. She exits the car and walks to the side entrance. As expected it is secured from within. White rose petals litter the sidewalk like shattered pieces of a broken dream. Upon returning to her vehicle, Alice sees the keys still in the ignition, the doors locked and impenetrable. It takes a skilled locksmith nearly an hour to come and open it for her.

Alice will not write Oscar Simon again; nor will she open anymore of his letters. A month later a courier knocks on the door and delivers a package. It is a white rose perfectly preserved in block of clear resin. With it an elegantly handwritten note on stationary bearing the name Toy Menagerie that reads: "May memory of this blossom be inspiration through darkest passage."   And Alice Be never did solve the mystery how Oscar Simon knew where she lived.

Alice trudges back up the stairs and along the dimly lit hallway, feeling within the passage presence of an overshadowing presence. Room 36 is just as she remembers--at least the bed covers represent refuge from strangeness of this place. Everything now so much like a dream that Alice wonders if she might awaken suddenly and find she has been sleeping for a hundred years. Upon turning off the lamp switch a peculiar numbness shoots along her arm, then a sense of floating, as an infinite network of invisible tentacles lift her bodily. In an instant she is accelerated through a bright corridor, witnessing explosive birth of suns and galaxies through firefly existence, all folding into a tunnel like a scroll rolled into darkness. The sensation not altogether unpleasant, a feeling of timelessness lacking locality, transported someplace else, and feeling she has been here before.

Once again Alice is in the Black Forest. Why here-- why this place? Kristen is also here watching her, changed in a way she cannot fully comprehend. A torso grown out of exposed roots bleeding from the earth, with flesh of bark, black and siliceous. Alice has just plucked the white flower growing between two roots and placed it in the cleft of her breasts. She knows already what Kristen will say, as though the scene rehearsed many times over.

"Why have you brought me back to this place?" She demands.

"You never left. Like me you have been here since the beginning."

"This is not possible! I had a life before, memories of being a child...a father and a mother."

"Before you were, I am; and have been waiting ever since."

"Then it was you all along! You are the Baron!"

"I am."

"Why did you sacrifice your wife?"

"I did not. I sacrificed myself so that we both might live as one. She was so lovely in my arms and near to death. I thought that if I could control the magic of this place there could still be a chance. It was on the *Night of Walpurgisnacht*, the moon full as sometimes it is on that night. I came here hoping to find salvation, only the magic stronger than ever I thought possible. I have been trapped here ever since."

"Then are you also now the magic in these woods?"

"I am not. I am prisoner to that magic."

Another presence looms suddenly over both of them. This is the dread always Alice has dreaded, the anger that has always so easily consumed her. Now she has no doubt of her truer nature, the place she has always been. The real lord of this domain stands monarch dividing night into night. A principality conjured by a dying sorcerer, trapping his own soul in a life in death realm where light changed to shadow. A place darkly beautiful where there is no end and no continuance, only night everlasting. She feels drawn into nadir of his collapsing existence, a desire for forgetfulness, her flesh changing, being consumed into the symbiotic entwining black roots, never to be alone again.

Then Alice's eyes meet those of Kristen, the eyes of one lost. Sadness in those eyes, a need this time she cannot ignore. In moment of compassion, she removes the white flower from bosom of her heart and presents it to Kristen. In doing so, she pricks her finger, allowing a droplet of blood to flow along the neck.

"This is all I have to give." She says, pressing the bloodied stem into Kristen's delicate hand.

"It is enough."

Kristen rises up unbound.

Another change has already begun, Alice drawn into eye of luminosity radiantly pure. Never has she witnessed or dreamed anything like this. She sees in distant passage grotesque visage of a lonely man surrounded by shattered pieces of light, unable to piece together the puzzle. She sees Samantha, who she refused to call by name, because of something it might mean, a meaning she could not embrace at the time, and perhaps not ever. She sees faces only vaguely familiar passing as fluttering wings. Some she knew, some she abused. All victims of her rage, none really deserving of her anger. She sees beyond rim of the universe her grandfather and grandmother changed beautiful in a way that defies elemental convention of time, and her father with them as a little boy again. She weeps because of acceptance found at last, for the peace, and for the release of so many burdens bound in fear. Then flash of blinding light, as a flaming javelin pierces into her soul! And Alice Be dies.

A sound in eternity whispers name once upon a time remembered: *"Alice Be, Alice Be."*

She opens her eyes to the stinging flare of a flashlight, altogether confused, uncertain if this only beginning of another dream.

"I asked if you are okay, Miss... Be."

This voice from another time summons her back into the living moment.

"W-what did you say?"

"You were in an accident." The voice says to her. "An ambulance is on the way. You hit pretty hard. Lucky you stuck into a soft snow bank and wearing a seat belt."

Alice's vision begins to clear. She is back in her car, a young clear-eyed State Highway Patrolman bending over, applying gauze to her forehead.

"What happened?"

"You sideswiped another car. Fortunately there are no severe injuries."   Alice reaches up to feel the wound where he applied the gauze.

"Don't worry," he says comfortingly, "it's only a minor cut. Could have been much worst-- another six feet and your car would have skidded off into a ravine. Yes mam, you are real lucky."

"The other driver..."

"A little shook-up like you, but everyone is just fine. I need to verify some information, if you don't mind. According to your licenses your name is Alice Be, age 36, presently a resident of Los Angeles County in California?"

"Yes, that's right officer. I am on my way to Denver to attend my father's funeral. My mother is meeting me there Sunday."

"That would be today. Now that it has stopped snowing and the plows running you should be able to make Denver City in less than an hour, as long as you and your car check out. My condolence for your loss, Miss Be, I am sure your father would be happy that his daughter still on earth."

"I have one question officer, are there any hotels on this stretch of road?"

"No, not until you reach the Denver outskirts. There used to be one not far from here just outside Idaho Springs, an old European style mansion, but it closed down several years back. Why do you ask?"

Just then the Vail Community Ambulance arrives, red and orange flashing lights, mingling weirdly with the blinking blue glow of a spinning bulb mounted atop the police cruiser. Alice's legs feel weak as she gets out of her car. Nevertheless, she is glad to be alive. Then she sees something against the white landscape at her feet nearly buried, very nearly lost to changing elements. It is matrix of a black flower with withered petals. Reaching down to pick it up, the petals disintegrate into fine dust swept into the mountain air; *this new testament to another beginning.*

"Are you sure you can stand and walk on your own Miss Be?"

"Yes, I'm fine. I'll be fine for the rest of my life. You may call me Elyssa. That's what father named me. And for the first time in my life I know why."

Alice Be glad for the snow. She is glad because of emptiness in sky; because there is still hope in the past, and for future promise. *In season all things designed in a matrix of rebirth.*

6

Song of Budgies

The Budgies arrive by Air Canada just in time. Labor Day weekend has already come and gone, leaving behind a sullen atmosphere over the city. Late summer still lingers in the parks and along the avenues of planted shrubs. But all know that fall comes quickly here, and that too soon the already fading greenery will change, replaced by rich autumn colors. And just as quickly those colors destined to melt into a barren landscape of winter cold.

Sonia wonders how susceptible are Budgies to cold weather. They are after all used to being sheltered from the elements, protected from harsh climates since their long journey began. Only two weeks earlier, they were in Paris, arriving from Turkey via what was once the famously romantic Orient Express. Weeks earlier they flitted freely in a collage of emerald shadows, camouflaged by an array of flowers, yellow, green, and blue, blending into the jungle fuse of their native Australia west of the Great Dividing Range. Their journey begins by being flown express delivery on an Air India flight from Sydney to Delhi. From here the exotic species transported by truck through rugged terrain of southern Pakistan to Islamabad, and then to Kabul. It is unclear if the Budgies flown by commercial airline or by a military transport from Kabul to Cairo in order to skirt the unfriendly tensions that still exist between Iraq and Iran. Upon reaching the northern Sudan, they skirt along several hundred-kilometers of dangerous highway that runs along the trickle of the Nile Basin. The Egyptians have a particular reverence for exotic birds, and would have taken special care to ensure the comfort of the species.

Sonia has never been to Australia, to India, to Afghanistan, or to Egypt, nor many of the other places these little birds have traveled. She grew up in Montreal, Canada after her parents emigrated from Tunisia. Sonia has traveled only to the secure region of her home city Tunis, and only just to visit close family. To think of going anywhere else in the Middle East makes her afraid. The borders beyond, although lased with exotic history, are in her mind places plagued by dangerous unrest.

Nevertheless, she has visited all these ancient lands through mind of adolescent imagination, still remembering vividly her father reading to his daughter stories based on interpretations from the Koran. Her child mind sees snake of the Nile as it curls toward Cairo near mouth of the Suez Canal, then south to Hurghada, believed the place where the Red Sea parted. From here the mountain of *Jabal Mousa*, named by the Jews Mount Sinai, where God spoke to the prophet Moses and writes upon stone slates the Ten Commandments.

Through these stories she has seen the ever-spreading deltas of modern irrigation fields of the Levant. The steep steps of Mount Ararat still clutching to this day the secret hulk of Noah's ark surrounded on all sides by guarded desolate borders. Iran, that most delicious queen of antiquity, nestled between Mesopotamia and greater Persia, waiting patiently since the fall of Media. From bosom of that luxurious pleasure dome sired Cyrus the Great, chosen of God, whose destiny is to crush through impenetrable gates of a once invincible empire, gutting open the ancient stronghold city of Babylon. Given vision through a divine dream, he commands the assimilated Jews to go out into the wilderness and rebuild Jerusalem. Darius the Great, made another King of Kings, who ruled the world for nearly half a century, followed by his son the magnificent Xerxes. This same Xerxes lead an army of millions said to have lapped small lakes dry during course of his invasion campaigns against the Greeks. And still to this day the ancient fires of vengeance continue to smolder in the ashes of those once great fallen empires.

Sonia's father also believed wholeheartedly in the historical validity of these places and events. He had archeologist friends commissioned on expeditions to verify old-culture myths found in the Bible, the Koran, and related documents. They accumulate actual photographic proof of coral-encrusted shapes strongly resembling Egyptian chariot wheels, along with many other artifacts scattered along bottom of the Red Sea. The bulk of their evidence considered insubstantial for modern scientific acceptance in light of Uniformitarian criterion. Nevertheless the documentation coincides with topographic models showing possible elevation depths and prevailing wind factors based on backward time predictions. This includes satellite telemetry, which reveals a shallow underwater ridge with deep troths on both sides connecting Egypt to Arabia where these artifacts found. By methodically piecing together all the elements, this group of rogue scientists introduces an irrefutable model challenging precepts of the status quo.

"It makes one reflect that because the shape and depth of water systems a certain way today, does not mean that always they were this way." Then gazing deeply into his daughter's eyes, Sonia's father reiterates. "Remember child that definition of a miracle is coincidence and timing of an event, which makes it no less miraculous. The mechanics of this world is a domino of existence too grand for mortal comprehension, yet already clearly designed from end to beginning in the mind and thoughts of God. Seek answers more in the patterns of disturbance, than just looking at the cause of an event."

Parting of the Red Sea does not stand alone in these Biblical archeologist's efforts to resurrect hidden mysteries of the past. Noah's Ark has tantalized story telling since even before the first level plane geometrically constructed foundations uncovered in Mesopotamia. The same events describing a global deluge that wipes out civilization found fragmented, yet preserved in unrelated cultures around the globe. These unassuming men of science recite repeatedly scientific data describing "*fault folding*" and "*rock strata displacement*". By interpreting the data differently, they point out inherent flaws to rigidly ascribed dating mechanisms relied upon by modern Uniformitarian scientist. Sonia's father becomes also convinced by many of their findings after reading a comprehensive volume written by John Whitcomb and Henry Morris titled *The Genesis Flood* published in 1961. This alternate interpretation using the same data incorporates modern satellite telemetry, which has actually captured from space what appears to be a manmade oblong object trapped under the ice on slopes of Mount Ararat. Although the Muslim version varies slightly in details and location, still the tantalizing possibility of such a structure surviving the course of civilized history fascinating.

Although met with the same abstinence of skepticism, it leaves stains of doubt in intellectual minds. As a backlash reaction, these discrepant finding labeled "*fringe*" and "*absurd*" for daring to challenge the rigidity of deterministic values. Even her father's career as a reporter tarnished, by daring to provide published validity of their collective research. Nevertheless, the collaboration of evidence proves to open minds of academia that at least some part of the ancient texts based on more than just superstition, inspiring Sonia to pursue a career in applied science to better determine basic truths underlying existentialism.

"The mind of myopias is such as to make some known facts definitive, and therefore more predictable than the extraordinary possibilities of potentials that might exist beyond confines of the local arena." He says to his only daughter in response to her growing inquisitiveness. "There is more to existence that we don't see, than the small percent that we do see. Remember this as your mind expands in knowledge. Even a simple equation is limited by context of the formulation, which ultimately becomes stumbling block to all reason."

Unlike Sonia's mother, her father's faith not steeped in religious contriteness. Even though he attends services regularly and observes high holidays, future vision for his daughter is not to just become a good Muslim wife as prescribed by tradition, but to become an equal in both mind and ability. Believing that life an analogy of all creation, he considers that all things biological, including children, are for a season given in the charge of their parents. But there comes a time when that child must choose independently what they will do and believe.

"As witnessed all around us, Sonia, this world has a natural course fulfilled through each species. But only children of men capable of making choices between good and evil, only men capable of violence for violence sake. This alone is the fulfillment of all meaning, not based solely upon biology. I believe it is by design of greater will that you be more than the sum of all you can be."

This does not mean her father did not believe in *Allah* or the *Hadiths* of the old prophets. As a younger man he had wanted to become a *Mullah*, but realized his calling in another direction. Rather, Sonia's father's God a presence more comprehensive than religion allows, a God merciful, capable of communicating through the elements of creation, with a voice above all prophets and all religions. To his friends, and even to his wife, this smacks against Islam, considered by many as beliefs sacrilegious!

To which he replies, gazing lovingly into his daughter's eyes, as only a father can.

"God did not make mankind in his image to be as mindless servants, but as children of creation. Even our scripture teaches us that we wait upon *Isa Masih* to come and restore all things. This anointed one is both, image of the elemental and image of the spiritual. Through measure of sacrifice and mercy, all have hope and promise. For it is written that *Isa Masih* will stand before the mercy seat as our advocate in the final judgment of all things. On that day there is not male, nor female; righteous, nor unrighteous; but all kneel condemned by the same condemnation, none saved or worthy except by hope in *Isa Masih*."

On September 11, 2011 his brother dies in a senseless attach on the New York World Trade Center. The older sibling was an accountant in an office located in the South Tower. Sonia's father weeps bitterly as he watches in horror the aftermath of the first plane, an American Airlines Jet Flight 11 that has already hit the North tower. Then the second plane, a United Airlines jet Flight 175, slams into the building where his brother worked igniting into a ball of fire. The next day Sonia's father hears from his brother for the last time by a haunting message left on his office answering machine.

"Are you covering what's happening here? It's like the *'Al-Malhama Al-Kubra!'* What in the name of Allah is that?" Then there is an increasing static crackling noise. "It is so beautiful-- as a shimmering bird of paradise! Pray for me my brother that this day I stand before *Isa Masih!"*

The roar of something large crashing through glass, bloodcurdling screams, and then there is only silence. They never did find the body of his lost brother.

Ten years later another disturbance resonates from the Middle East, which will be known as the Arab Spring. It begins with civil war in Sonia's homeland of Tunisia, quickly spreading into border countries. Being a journalist, as well as a man of personal principle, her father accepts a volunteer assignment to Libya. Sonia's mother was against him going, saying that she and his family ought to come first. Although not a man of radical idealism, he was a man who believed in future value of democracy and who loved the lands of his nativity.

"Maybe this is an awakening," he says passionately before leaving on that fateful journey. "I only hope that after the fires die-out something better might be established in place of the corrupt indulgent monarchies that now rule through division."

The man Sonia most loved and respected in memory killed early in life, buried on a pleasant hill near his birthplace outside Tunis, his body facing right of Mecca according to custom. She was already twenty four at the time and living in her own apartment located in the west end of town to be near her new job as a University teaching assistant at McGill. Her father's funeral unearthed another unexpected revelation. Turns out Sonia had a brother two sisters from a previous union. According to religion a Muslim man is entitled to more than one spouse. Fortunately, they all get along splendidly, destined to reunite as extended family in future years. Feeling some resentment, as some part of her would have liked to have known, remembering how lonely she felt at times growing up without siblings. These thoughts she keeps hidden and to herself in respect to the wishes of her parents.

Also Sonia will remember always the sadness, the constant wailing of her mother that lasted for more than a month. During those first weeks, they went often to the Mosque to pray, rarely speaking about the past, never about the future. Until one day her mother packs all her father's things and donates them to charity. Now only a few pictures of Sonia's father remain in the house, a ghostly reminder that once her mother married, as always she avoids mentioning his name for fear of the pain it causes.   And for the next several years there will remain in her mother's home rooms she never turns on the lights, places of outer darkness shut up and sealed in her heart.

Sonia's mother had encouraged her daughter to marry what she considered an ideal prince from Saudi Arabia named Omar, whose family got rich doing business with the west. Although appealing to future expectation (mostly those of her mother), Omar fulfilled the worst prophecy of Arab Muslim men, believing women servitude, mostly existing for his pleasure and future progeny. After a union lasting less than two years, it is discovered that Sonia unable to bare children. Therefore the deal called off, leaving Sonia with only two choices: taking position as a second wife, or divorce. So Sonia chooses divorce.

She dates a few men over the next several years, some Muslim and some not. She realizes over time that most Muslim men have the same expectation as Omar, with little appreciation for Sonia's intellect and scholastic achievements, none possessing the cherished wisdom of her father. By now she has a fulltime teaching schedule, even traveling to places like Japan and European countries to speak at seminars, already with reputation as one of the leading intellects in her field. On one such excursion she meets David Gray, a wealthy Englishman. David is handsome and charming, in every way the perfect image of another fairy book prince. His hair shone silver blond in the sun, his eyes as light, which contrasted wonderfully with the almond brown of Sonia's eyes and the raven black of her hair. He was light and she was shadow, the perfect combination of a dream.

From the beginning his presence intoxicating, opening something deep within Sonia's physical body, allowing many pent-up emotions to seethe to the surface. She was usually more disciplined than this, more capable of hiding her true feelings. She allows herself to imagine, as women usually do, of what it would be like to live in a mansion with servants, surrounded by luxury, and with David Gray at her side. But then reality begins cracking to the surface. It turns out that David Gray has a litany of ex-wives, often drinks too much, and frightened by the depth of deep emotional commitment. And as Sonia's mother points out, the fact he refuses even to consider converting to Islam makes him an inadequate choice. Secretly Sonia might have conceded to this last demand, had David been able to allow himself to truly love. She would mourn the loss of this relationship more than any she had in the past, and it would be many months before braving those depths of emotion again. Now an accepted professional, her work the central core of Sonia's existence, what possible logic was there to get tangled into another complicated relationship involving feelings?

It is inevitable that Sonia drawn to Leo, a man with ways of thinking so much like her father. Leo is in every way opposite to Omar or to David Gray. He is not tall or handsome, nor is he even Muslim, but a Jew, son of Holocaust survivors, who proclaims pedigree of neither religion, nor social prestige. A licensed psychologist by profession, he tends to live more a life of philanthropy, with a knack for wheeling and dealing. Being the only son of a haggardly couple originally from Belgium, who survived the atrocity of the Dachau Concentration Camp at end of the Second World War, later immigrating to Canada. Leo's father became a Tailor, opening his own business, but wanted better for his son, so made sure Leo went to university and obtain a professional degree. Sonia met the couple only once at their favorite hangout at a McDonald's on Queen Mary Road. From this solitary meeting she understands why Leo the way he is.

Sonia cannot say really what about Leo attracts her. He has tendency at times to say crude things, which seems out of character in the moment, yet makes her laugh unexpectedly. Sometimes Leo is as scholarly and spiritual as her father, and other times a total buffoon. Even Sonia's mother likes Leo and with the same perplexity of the why. But there is something about this man painfully sensitive, something that draws-in emotional response from both Sonia and her mother, creating an oasis of comfort within. He speaks honestly and from the heart, with the expressiveness of a neglected child. Sonia might have considering marrying Leo for this solitary reason. Not an attraction based on love or desire (at least not as she loved and desired David Gray), but because of a greater need to fulfill a void of emptiness inside, the same emptiness that she often feels. Again her mother questions: *Would he, being a Jew, ever convert to Islam?*

When asked, Leo responds as might Sonia's father were he still alive.

"In your religion you believe Abraham to be your patriarch, as do the Jews. You also believe God spoke to Moses from smoke of a burning mountain, as do the Jews. You believe in the laws of Moses, and promise of a Messiah sent by God, as do the Jews. Although our religious instruction differs, the meaning is the same. To be honest, Sonia, neither of us is really all that much religious. But we do share belief in something that provides meaning to mortal passage, an awareness of purpose that many in this world do not know. To truly believe in the essence of our religion is the belief in the one true God above all other gods, be this God named *YHWH*, *HaShem*, or *Allah*. And since both our religions profess deliverance through an appropriated Messiah, rather called by name *Isa Mesih*, *Yeshua*, or *Yeshua HaMashiah*, then we are made living witnesses to an unbelieving world. You and I both are in professional positions where existentialism and atheism the norm for many great minds. These are our friends and colleagues, people we know and care about in earthly passage. How can we share with them the meaning of faith without first having faith in the source of that meaning? To convert to anything Sonia would be to deny truth sewn before there was an earthly institution collectively embraced named religion."

Sonia's mother ceases to ask Leo to convert after this. In time they become more than friends, something less than committed lovers. Leo exists in her mind like a comfortable pair of shoes or a worn-out sweater she likes wearing when there is a nip in the air. He exhibits selfless effort in consideration of her exhaustive work schedule. Although he demands more of her time than makes Sonia comfortable, Leo accepts being second place to her driven need to succeed in very a competitive work place. And although they often disagreed, even on the smallest details, she could never imagine him not being there. Then one day two years after the death of his mother and father, Leo decides to liquidate all his earthly assets and journey out into straits of the greater world.

"Why must you go away?" Sonia demands, determined to keep concealed the alarming depth of her sadness.

"Now it is just me and my sister left, and she wants nothing to do with family ties or family inheritance outside her marriage. Besides, you will achieve your dream of getting Tenor soon. This is what you always wanted, and what I want for you."

"Maybe less important than sometimes I think. I must confess Leo that I have had dreams of letting everything go and just find simplicity without all the stress."

"We both know you could never do that Sonia. Your accomplishments are evident of the person you are; the gift your father always wanted his daughter to be. I could never take that away from you, Sonia. No love can be greater than the love of sacrifice. This love I also leave with you now."

When Sonia turns forty-five she finally receives Tenor at the university, which means she can now relax in job security and in accolade of professional achievement. This is how the Budgies come into her life; a gift from Leo delivered to the university faculty office by special courier with a note attached.

"From the first day I met you I knew you to be special as a beautiful bird sent from heaven. According to your tradition, it is said that the people of the mountains once wandered through the earth as nomads. They prayed to God to give them a home. The good lands had already been promised to others, so God gave them a strait to the moon. Here the people have lived ever since; content to be in the land that God has provided. Birds are sent as free angels to remind us of habitations between the earth and the moon. When they sing among us, we know it is the sound of blessing. And when they fly away, a part of us goes with them, as part of their song remains within us. They are the promise of greater hope to come. Abiding witness of what our two religions call "*God's Chosen One*" through different language and culture. I have become a *Wandering Jew*, but my heart remains empty every place I go. Still I remember the song you made in my life, and often I think of what it might be like to return. In the meantime, dear Sonia, I send you this gift of Budgies to sing always in your heart. For greater is the sound of music, than words of the song."

Sonia would not see Leo again, but when her Budgies sang she thought about him. They talk sometimes on the phone, and inquiries to mutual friends keep her informed of his whereabouts. Leo will reside in Cuba for a time, but find nothing to keep him there. From here he travels to Panama, then to Brazil, and finally to Ecuador, where he settled for a while in the mountain city of Quito. As he predicted, Leo has become the true embodiment of a *Wandering Jew,* always looking for place to call home, but never finding it.

To her knowledge Leo died alone in a hotel room after a minor hernia surgery. Sonia would never receive a clear answer as to what happened. Time passes and each morning and each evening the Buggies sing, keeping Sonia in pleasant memory of life's more wonderful gifts. Then one morning eight years later, Sonia awakens to the sound of only one bird. A sound it has never made before. On the floor of the cage lies its companion, stiff and lifeless. Lifting the body of faded feathers gently in her hand, Sonia begins to weep. She weeps for the years gone by, for all the love she missed, and all the love she missed to give. She weeps for her father, who chose to see his daughter as an individual equal to all others despite prejudice of conditioning. She weeps for the love she suffered in arms of a rich man, who made her dream for a moment of castles in the sky. But most Sonia weeps for Leo, a man who could never find peace on this earth and now sings a chorus surrounded by multitudes somewhere else, no longer contained to a distant flickering universe. This moment Sonia embraces the meaning of her remaining Budgie's song, a simple melody to remind the world that all things temporal, all things made mutable, and that even the grand spinning galaxies but firefly existences in the eye of eternity. And in this solitary moment, Sonia realizes the truest measure of love.

Later in life, Sonia would end up marrying a colleague of many years at the University Faculty Office where she has worked nearly all her life. They share much in common, the same profession, the same work schedule, which keeps daily life simple. She will love this man, as an accomplished peer deserving of her respect, as true to love as Sonia will ever know. Her mother will accept him as well, because he is Muslim, born from the same region, which she thinks makes him also predictable. Both Sonia and her husband dream of pleasant retirement and one day returning to Tunisia, where they have purchased a house with a garden. And in this garden stands an empty cage inhabited once upon a time by pair of singing Budgies in a past now only vaguely remembered.

7

Cloud Rider

There is a place above the clouds of Olympus where spirits and angels join in a game of eternity," Grandfather says to me and my baby brother, holding us tightly. "They are called Cloud Riders. And this, Athia, is why the Greek people are never forgotten, no matter what happens here on the earth."

"What kind of game, grandfather?" I ask.

"What kind of game? Child--the game of hopes and dreams-- the stuff we are all made of! It is this game that gives light to our souls and purpose to our existence. Because you are special, I have given you the special name Athia. I will also tell you another secret that few in this passage will ever know: *Life is a fisherman of illusion; and time the net of patience*. And the Cloud Riders slip streams between heaven and us, surfing the wind of suns beyond rim of what we can see."

Mask of Her Reflection in Venus

   This man of wondrous reflection remains in my mind the voice of an ancient Seer of Delphi surrounded in twilight. The shadow of his haggard face as a roadmap of life, his favorite briar pipe a magic wand wedged tightly in a strong hand, and with eyes as sparkling shards from distant stars gazing out an open window. Always I felt protected in his warm presence; always I felt loved.

   This special name given to me by grandfather I have gone by even before I learned to read. He said it was a name from somewhere else, which means "*Istunus*", because of something written in my eyes. I will later learn that the word is originally Latin, meaning "*One Just*", a name I have gone by for nearly all my life. One of the first words spoken from the mouth of my little brother, Nicolas, was my new name Athia. Because they liked it better than my given name, mother and father also begin calling me Athia. By the time I start school, my teachers and my friends all refer to me as Athia.

   Grandfather was a simple man, not particularly educated, who worked at a job unloading ships somewhere near a city named Piraeus. But he read a lot, with particular interest in Classical Greek literature, which he considered metaphor of modern world history. He could have been a scholar, but chose to remain humble to the necessities of his family. He and grandmother often babysat my brother and me when mother had to work late. They felt it their duty as parents to their youngest daughter-in-law to help out as much as possible. I think that secretly they liked having children in the house again and cherished our presence as much as we appreciated being there.

   Early memories of grandmother are that she was less the dreamer and more domestic. It is she that made sure we did our homework, brushed our teeth after eating a hardy supper prepared by her own hand, and ready by the time my mother arrived to pick us up. Recollection of this

time in my life remains vivid to this day, a time of affection
and dreams, still innocent to the ways of this world.
Grandmother was also more religiously spiritual, sharing a
certain affinity with my little brother often making me feel
deprived.

Young Nicolas even then was far too sensitive for a
boy. I think that secretly he wished for another name as
well. He just never felt like a Nicolas, a name too strong in
his mind. He should have been born the girl; allowed to be
whatever it was he felt. His favorite pastime was lying
dreamily on a hill making romantic stories in the clouds
about beautiful princesses kissed by a prince, and what it
like to dress in satin and sparkling high heel shoes. He
played more often with my dolls than I did. Whereas, I am
the one always climbing trees, getting my knees skinned-
up from too much rough activity. I think that Nicolas was
more than a little jealous of my new name as we got older.
Jealous because I would mature to become beautiful like
our mother, and because he knew that inside I was more
of a boy than he. And perhaps, if the truth were to be
known, Nicolas was more feminine than anyone in our
family wished to admit.   My brother would eventually come
out and be considered openly gay; but even this
description not completely adequate to describe what
Nicolas really felt within. Despite the jealousy--and often
judgments--my brother and I loved each other more than
words can express. Nicolas remains my best friend to this
day--a friendship that defies even the grave.

These early memories of childhood are mixed with
fanciful tales mixed with the sound of grandfather's voice
relating to father events when he was a young man. He
suffered along with all of the Mediterranean countries
following German invasion. This before father born, before
the world changed to what it is today, and before the
German war machine carved Greece into three factions.
This hungry beast appropriated most of the resources and

grounded the fishing fleets, causing hard times to the native population. Grandfather claims that people resorted to eating grass and insects. By the second year of the invasion hundreds of thousands of souls perished in a winter remembered in history as the *Great Greek Famine*. In 1943 my grandfather and his older brother joined one of the underground resistance groups, becoming part of a movement to establish a *"Free Greece"* in the mountains. I can see the horror in his eyes, a dead place in my heart of my father's father, a place without light or forgiveness, even for himself. Father actually cried one night upon hearing how the uncle he never knew, except from faded black and white photographs, died of a fever because there was no medicine available to save him.

I also cried, but eventually forgave my grandfather for these terrible images of war, followed later with civil unrest caused by the Communist to create divisions of ethnic cleansing.   Images I wish to this day to close my eyes to-- preferring the classical richness of gods and angels playing games in heaven. Not that I believed these to be more real, only more palpable to my child imagination. All this terrible suffering happened long before Nicolas and I were born. Yet somehow there remains a shadowy dormancy of this genetic history that cannot be expressed in words, but exist as an imprinted reminder of what civilized society capable of.

My father grew up in a Greece divided. The socialist on one side fighting for unions and better living conditions for the poor, continued news reports of territorial disputes mostly on the Yugoslavia border to the north, and Greece's slow ascension into the European post-war economic community spurred on by the Marshall Plan. Father was not particularly political, nor did he embrace the idea of a European Common Market. By the time my brother and I born, tourism had become a central infusion of Athens' economic prosperity. It was not unusual to see people from all over the globe browsing through the shops and market places in out of the way suburbs.   However, this new wave of world tourism also meant that Athens no longer belonged to Athenians. Even though we lived only a few miles from the ancient site of the Greek Acropolis, I will be a teenager before allowed to visit it.

"I will not pay even one Drachma to visit a place where I played free as a child! It is my birthright and the birthright of my children!" Father swore often every time a new levee imposed.

As a consequence we knew less about the foundations of our own history than the average tourist from America. Mother, on the other hand, was more cosmopolitan. Being the daughter of an aristocrat, her family had escaped the austerity of conditions imposed by the New Order of German domination. Fleeing first to Crete across the Aegean Sea, and then to British controlled Palestine, they had been immune to the terrible suffering, later raising their only daughter in post-war prosperity. As a result, our mother possessed an optimism, which provided emotional balance to our family existence.

We lived at this time in a small apartment just above an outside vegetable market in Kolonaki, which was also home to a colony of mice that persistently found their way behind the cooking stove. Mother was constantly complaining, constantly setting traps, and constantly sealing cracks and crevices believed to be their points of entry. In time the mice stopped getting in; or else became wiser, making their presence less obvious. There were several brothels in our neighborhood, which we were instructed as children to ignore. It was not unusual to see a drunken patron clutched in the arms of a prostitute.

"Come along children", my mother would hastily say without comment or distraction, pretending this to be a normal practice on the streets in our neighborhood.

Mask of Her Reflection in Venus

It was my mother, who also provided a dimension of culture to our family. She insisted upon taking Nicolas and me to the Opera and to museums that were free. On occasions father even came with us. Not because he liked the events, but because he enjoyed these special outings with his family. It was one of the few times I saw my father and mother really dressed up. They made a handsome couple, father in his stylish Fedora hat and sporting a hand-carved wooden cane; and with mother at his side like a bright painted Cézanne flower blossoming beneath the shade of her broad-rimed sunhat. I imagined how elegant a couple they must have made on their wedding day. The photos of that event lost in a fire a few days before I was born. Sometimes we would embark on a nearly two hour drive in sweltering traffic to visit an aunt living on the outskirts of Corinth and go swimming at a nearby beach named Kalamia. This was an area my father spent much of his prowling days before meeting his wife, representing a freedom lost to his carefree nature. I think mother found these excursions less interesting, only submitting to the long day as she did to any other wifely duty.

My aunt was a robust woman, who always kept a supply of Ouzo stashed in the freezer. First thing on the agenda was for her and father to take a shot. This ritual repeated many times through the course of a day. However, mother always intervened at least two hours before our scheduled departure, stating strongly that her safety and the safety of her children paramount. Although father grimaces, he acquiesces to this voice of sound reason, and the Ouzo returned to the freezer, until next visit.

"You children don't realize how fortunate you are!" My aunt often reminds us upon our departure. "History of the Greek people has not always been easy. First the Romans, then invasion by the Turks, followed by Nazi Fascist, and now the Communist-- each taking their turn to suckle the rich milk of our land. Still the Greek spirit continues to survive! We were the first to provide the world a definition of civilization, and in return our culture pillaged; our lives made to bleed into the Aegean without so much as a thank you! But you represent future of a better world. Never forget the rich pool of your nativity. Even the gods are children of God."

She would then hug us goodbye, as we suffocated in the flesh of her large breast. Of course, at the time I had little appreciation for what she was saying. There was something sad about my aunt that I could never completely identify. Being my father's only sister, she tends often to complain about what they lacked growing up, expressing open jealousy for her brother's present happiness. Perhaps her greatest sadness was that at child-bearing age she became a young widow, when her husband died tragically in a road accident. Or perhaps because she was more intelligent than women were supposed to be then, preferring to read books about history, rather than chat idly about fashion and domestic prosperity of the times. She would never remarry, destined to die childless at an early age from alcohol related live failure. I wish now that I had spent more time speaking with her, learning from lips of this woman of modern comprehension the acquired wisdom of a world unique to her generation.

I remember one Saturday morning particularly well when we plan a lunch at the *Doric Temple of Apollo*. We found a suitable hill slopping opposite to the seven Hellenistic limestone columns marking the ruins. We would have preferred spreading our blanket and dine within the foundation of this pastoral landmark, except there were several cars and two buses crowding the entrance.

"Tourist-- so many tourists-- and here we must visit our own history by remaining on the outside!" Father complains.

Mask of Her Reflection in Venus

"Without them we would have nothing." Mother says soothingly. "At least we have bread and cheese on our table every day, and wine for the stomach. It is better to be full of crumbs, than to be empty through pride of tradition. It is good that they come and we eat than not eat at all for lack at the grocery store."

Father only nods his head without challenge, accepting the sound reason of his wife, as he accepts all the things in the world he knows, but cannot change. Another time, when Nicolas and I still adolescents, we went on a family camping trip, staying the night at a local campground called *Dionisiotis*. I would later learn that the name was a derivative of *Dionysos*, the God of wine, often depicted as half man and half animal.   Something terrifying happened that night, something mythological and beyond the capacity of my young mind to comprehend. Even to this day, I am only vaguely certain if what I saw real, the lingering remnants of a bad dream, or a concoction of both conjured through childhood imagination. We were staying in a refurbished Army tent Father picked up from a friend at work, packed side by side like sardines in the cocoon of blankets brought for the occasion.   Sometime after midnight I awoke with an urgent need to pee. I crept a small distance away from the tent, squatting near a fence erected at the end of the campground. I no sooner finish, when I hear a heavy breathing sound from behind, feeling the exhale of hot breath on the back of my neck. Spinning around, I see a large dark figure standing erect and looming on the other side of the mesh. It seemed more like an animal hunched on two legs, than a human apparition. Particularly remarkable were its two red eyes, as embers of burning coals in a smoldering oven. I quickly race back to the safety of our tent enclosure and snuggle my head beneath the covers until morning light filters into the forested basin, chasing away the shadows of the previous night. Next morning, I share the vision with my brother.

"What you saw was probably one of the old gods of Greece." Nicolas affirms, having begun reading a book about the gods of mythology. "They weren't always good, you know. They are imagined as happy beings that come to help mortals, but are in reality demons. The true Dionysus often took young virgins for his own pleasure. You are special Athia, and that is why God has sent us to always protect each other. No matter what happens in life, or who I might one day become, always remember that I am a part of you."

Since that night Nicolas has remained my only best friend. Not that we never disappointed one another, but always loyal to each other no matter where we went or what we did. Nicolas is still my Hercules with sword drawn to slay all demons. I lost all interest in going camping after that night.

I had just turned fifteen when grandfather came to live in our house. Grandmother died suddenly, peacefully in her bed. The doctors said it due to age and that her heart just gave out. She was such a kind soul, a woman faithful to the needs of everyone around her. Raised Orthodox, grandmother always engaged community activities and volunteered regularly at the church. If not for the presence of this woman we may have all gone heathen. And even though she kneeled often at the throne of heaven, she is the rod that kept grandfather grounded in the present. Without her quiet guidance he was like a confused child always looking for something lost on earth, only oblivious to what that something is. So mother and father move him into a spare room prepared in the cellar where the vegetable bin and the wine kept. Grandfather liked wine, so he did not mind so much as long as he had free-range to rest of the house.

Less than a year later, he began sleeping more than usual, less engaged, and increasingly lethargic. Then one morning, like grandmother we woke up to find him dead with a Bible once belonging to his wife opened to the scripture in First Corinthians that reads: *"In a moment, in the twinkling of an eye, at the last trumpet. For the trumpet will sound, and the dead will be raised incorruptible, and we shall be changed."*

A few days after the funeral I sat in our backyard, annoyed by a persistent bee that kept buzzing around my head. Then to my surprise it lights upon the back of my hand without stinging. For several moments we just look at each other. Then breath of a pleasant breeze lifts it into the air not to return. I know in my heart it was grandfather sending me a message that he was okay. His way of saying *"I am now a Sky Rider, as will you someday be."* I suppose this made his death easier in my mind. I later share this event with Nicolas. He too agrees that grandfather now part of everything and that he and grandmother are back together again.

"At least they won't never be lonely ever." Nicolas says with childish affection. "I wish one day we can all ride the clouds together."

After this I stop thinking of myself as being particularly special. I suppose that before this I imagined I would be the only one to slip the streams between heaven and earth, now aware of even greater potential. It is about this time that Nicolas tells me he likes dressing-up as a girl. At first I laugh, asking why he would want to wear dresses when he did not have to.

"Because I like dresses and just feel more myself that way. Ever since I can remember I have imagined myself as a girl. But Athia-- you must promise not to say anything to mom and dad! Please it is our secret."

"Of course, it will always be a secret just between us. I often felt there was something different about you. I am glad it is something not terrible. I can help you maybe with your hair and makeup."

Nicolas and I start going out to parties together, except now I introduce him as my sister Nicoletta. Nicoletta becomes quite popular, especially with the boys. This is concerning to me, since I know how boys can be. I become watchful of my younger sibling to the point of acting like a chaperone bodyguard. In time mom and dad find out our secret, but accept Nicoletta as a second daughter. I think this was perhaps more difficult for father, because he always felt proud to have a son. Even though laws in Greece more lax now concerning sexual diversity, it became increasingly uncomfortable as Nicolas, now Nicoletta began acting and living more openly in her new chosen identity. Neighbors we knew for years, whose children we played with while growing up, now close their doors to our presence. I must admit that this feeling of rejection was the worst part of it. But Nicoletta suffered the most, often locking her room and crying for days.

At nineteen I begin seriously dating a boy originally from the town of Corfu. His name is Lucas, which he says means *"bringer of light"*, second son of an Egyptian family originally from Cairo. He is smart, well educated, and also naturally good at most things once he puts his mind to it. I decide not to tell Lucas that Nicoletta is not a sister, but actually my brother thinking it simpler this way. I think he suspected something different about Nicoletta, especially when often mother or I made a slip-up and call Nicoletta he or him, instead of she or her. He never says anything, but I can tell by the arch of his eyebrow that he is pondering the deeper meaning. I think that if the truth told, Lucas knew even then, only deciding to remain discreet, which is characteristic of his better nature.

It happened in late summer of the same year Lucas and I announced our engagement. I had already started a modeling career, considered photogenic in the industry, and already making my own money. With both their children grown and now living away from home, father and mother have chosen to live separate, saying only that their interests have changed. Nicoletta has since taken up the guitar and lives with a roommate on the Aegean coast outside of Katerini.

Now Nicoletta goes by the name Niki, and since last seeing her, has joined a touring Christian rock band named *Elysium*. Lucas thinks the idea of Christian rock bordering on sacrilegious, unbecoming of the acculturated Coptic beliefs practiced by his family. Personally, I like the spirituality I feel when listening to them play. It is hard to believe that Niki is the same little brother I knew as a child, so similar, yet unlike that little boy with such beautiful clear blue eyes. Nor is Niki anything like Nicoletta, who always struggled so hard to be accepted as a girl. This version of my sibling more peaceful than I have ever known, now confident in a way that I cannot help but envy just a little.

"You look beautiful Athia," Niki says tearfully falling on my neck. "I have had so many wonderful dreams about you and the many memories we shared growing up."

"So what has happened to Nicoletta?"

"She is still here, but so is your brother Nicolas. We are in balance since the day I found the Lord and filled with the Holy Spirit. When I was a child I felt jealousy because grandfather gave you your special name. And later as you grew into such a beautiful woman I wanted to be as you. But now I know what I did not know then. In this world I am made divided, often feeling split in half. In the resurrection there is neither male nor female, but we will all be as angels before the throne of God. Because I am loved for who I am, then I am able to love me also, and love you as never I have loved before."

"I have always loved you just the way you are."

"I know Athia." Niki says with a hint of sad awareness. "It is for this reason we will ride the clouds forever together.

Always remember this even in the darkest night. Remember that strength is not what me think or pretend to be. It is through meaning of what we are made to be."

I am unsure at the time what Niki really means. All that I know is that in the moment it was like having my brother back. We weep and laugh together that whole afternoon. Niki, Nicolletta, Nicolas-- all three rolled into one. This was my brother, my sister, and my friend. There would never be another person like this person. This is also what makes this story joyful even in face of tragedy.

According to testimony, Niki goes swimming with some friends while touring the Crete Island near Elounda. At evening he fails to return with the group. When my little brother younger, he did so love the water, so loved to ride the currents wherever they might lead. They never did find the body even after a search lasting many days. For a time I weep inconsolably. Why had God taken someone so young and beautiful? Someone that promised to make the world a better place just by being here!

A few months after burying an empty coffin, I sit alone upon a small hill in an empty park just before moonrise near where my new husband and I now live. The night sky as black velvet encrusted with myriad sequel of glittering stars. This moment so astounding that for an instance I forget the bearing of mortality. Then one of those stars begins moving closer and closer, until only its light fills my vision.

This moment I am touched by a presence never completely embraced before. I begin weeping, my soul pouring into the emptiness of a void fixed between distant points of light. I weep for the suffering witnessed by generation of my grandfather and grandmother ensnared in a web of violent upheaval that unmasks the worse face of humankind. I weep for mother and father, who sacrificed so much until their family old enough to understand, and wonder if they are truly happier now? I weep for Nicolas, also born Nicoletta, whose greater peace came only near the end. But I weep most because now I know also what Niki was trying to say to me that last day we shared together. It was never about the vanity of being, about positions of strength and weakness, or even complex strategies of survival. It is all about love from the beginning. This is what makes the human spirit different, and why it is fashioned humble in the face of prevailing mortality: *for to love at expense is the truest measure of what love means.*

I name my first child Niki, as hope for a better and more prosperous Greece. Not just the Greece of past history, but a nation with a future soul. Still there will always remain in my mind those many impressionable memories of my own childhood. These were the simple times, times shared in hope by families everywhere in the world. A time remembered in the past, when torn nations buried their dead to construct dreams of a better world. A time nearly forgotten, before Greece rose out of the ashes of antiquity, resurrected as a model for future generations. This phoenix of historical and future reference knitted tightly into the fabric of global communities, whose influence continues to spread in all directions beyond its white shores.

Father was right about many things, but what he was most right about is that all things change. Greece changed much after the Second World War, as has much of the world since. But the things that remain changeless are recollections pleasant and unpleasant stored memorial in the heart. And always when I look up into the sky I see Niki with grandfather and grandmother surfing together upon billowing clouds. Truly free at last, they exist in a stream of time divided by time, surfing the winds forever, as I wish to traverse the heavens with them. And often I wonder to myself how long before I am born again a Cloud Rider.

8

Blind Osiris

Hannah always greatly admired her Uncle Jeremiah. So much that she determines to follow in his steps by pursuing a career in archeological science. She remembers as a child crouched at his feet while he and father discussed subjects profoundly interesting. Things that she could not even comprehend at the time, yet stirred within her some latent curiosity that makes her dream of things impossible. Uncle Jeremiah was born blind in one eye, a condition he tries often to conceal, particularly evident when he would look down searching the shadows for his niece.

Hannah's father, conservative in his way of thinking, relies more on what he calls "*Scientific Evidence*". For this reason the two men rarely readily agree on any subject, especially when Uncle Jeremiah begins speaking on topics considered by most experts to be outlandish theories about ancient gods and the world that was before the Great Flood in the days of Noah. His brother would physically cringe when Jeremiah began one of his often rants about Hitler's links with the Occultist Thule Society. Jeremiah is convinced that sudden technological rise of the Third Reich to military superiority due to the acquisition of ancient knowledge contained within certain artifacts no longer part of human consciousness.

"But something they did not find-- something they wanted so badly that had they found it would have changed the outcome of everything. There is still more death heads to be unleashed from inside Pandora's Box. I'm certain of it!"

"The only thing certain is that the Nazis hated Jews and tried to exterminate as many as they could!" Her father bellows.

"Yes, Samuel, they did. But the question you should ask yourself is why? Why Jews the target of their primary focus? I think it because they are God's chosen people instilled with an awareness planted and nurtured by the author of creation. The real enemy is not mankind, but the mind of spirits that inhabit mankind."

"The devil made me do it is only an excuse. The mind and the hands still belong to men. And to such men there is no excuse!"

Hannah's father, only eleven months less a day older, shares little of his brother's analytical perspective of those early years when the Fascist took over Germany. Perhaps because his memories of that time more personal and therefore more vivid, he harbors the pain of many unhealed wounds. He still feels the stab of rejection by people he thought his friends then. A girl he liked changing her affections, accusing him of being inferior because he lacked Aryan blood. It is not that his pain greater, only the memory of that pain which refuses to go away.

Nevertheless, they both lost relatives to the Concentration Camps. Both spared a similar fate only because their parents wise enough to immigrate before the worst nature of mankind overshadowed Europe. Arriving first in Canada, and then moving to the U.S. they lived their early years as vagabond Jews in search of a permanent place to settle. The grandfather Hannah never knew remains in both their minds a rudder of guiding principle, impressing upon his two sons the unwavering principal that in light of the Holocaust atrocities, Jews ought to have a homeland as promised by God in the beginning. Now only these two brothers left: one convinced by doctrine of Modern Zionism that the strength of a well armed Israel the only answer; the other believing that by faith in divine intervention God's deliverance sure, as always has been the case with God's chosen people. And although only the two brothers now remain, often divided by memories and politics, the thing they most share most in common is survivor's guilt neither ever wants to talk about.

These darker events of history are rarely spoken aloud and only quietly shared by Hannah's mother. Her lineage different, tracing back to Ashkenazi emigrants forced to flee Russia on foot, an exodus nearly a century earlier after the Warsaw Pogrom, forcing expulsion of more than two million Jews. At least they were able to walk out on their own feet; even if many did die on the trail. Still it was better than being rounded-up and slaughtered like livestock in human processing facilities.

"It seems that in every century there are those who want to blame the Jews for the world's problems." Hannah's mother says often. "They justify themselves by saying it is because the Jews responsible for the murder of Christ. Yet, they murder us contrary to the teachings of Christ. In the end it all comes down to the same reason why Cain murdered his brother Abel. The blood of jealousy has flowed into the veins of earth ever since."

Mask of Her Reflection in Venus

Hannah rarely speaks much when her uncle comes to visit, preferring to just listen, as he shares with her father all the wonderful things he has seen and done during his travels abroad. In his early years, her uncle had studied to be a Rabbi, strongly interested in Theology. Then something happened in his life, which he describes as a spiritual incursion, causing him to renounce traditional religious teachings and to embrace for a time the eastern philosophy of Buddhism. No longer eligible for position of Rabbi, he turns to Archeology and Anthropology instead, inspired with zeal to prove a connection between spiritual belief and scientific data interpretation. He argues that there is less contradiction than superficially presented through bias of institutional acceptance. He becomes a true *savant* in every sense of the meaning, not content to just enrich his mind with principals of mechanical observation, but endeavors to discover logical connection between empirical observation and matrix of a microstructure, which he refers to as source of "*unquantifiable energy*".

Although her father a man of fewer convictions and expressing less faith, he always accepts his younger brother in their home with open arms. And even though they may disagree often-- *sometimes even vehemently on many subjects*-- always they part hugging one another affectionately, vowing that no difference able to break their bond of brotherhood.

As a respected archeologist, Jeremiah's work takes him to faraway places in the world, places of different cultures that inspire curiosity in young Hannah's imagination. Often Hannah secretly takes notes and later looks up these places in the family encyclopedia collection. After awhile, she begins to recognize the historical roots and topography of the places her uncle has been, and so often references in conversation. One evening after turning seventeen and preparing for her first semester at

UCLA, a light goes off in Hannah's mind and she dares to interrupt their after dinner reverie with her first truly meaningful inquiry.

"Uncle Jeremiah, why do you think the Pyramids originate from a time before recorded history; and that these architectures somehow designed to focus energy?"

Jeremiah and her father pause in mid-sentence. They are in the throes of a heated debate about the pyramids of Ancient Egypt and their possible meaning within modern context. It never occurs to either of them that she might be listening, much less comprehending the elevated content of their discussion. Both men only stare silently at each other astonished.

"Hannah you ought not to bother your Uncle Jeremiah with silly questions." Her father reprimands.

"No, Samuel, Hannah's question is not at all silly." Then turning to his niece, he says: "You are a most inquisitive young lady, Hannah, to be so attentive as to ask a question that even few academics brave enough to consider. In my generation girls rarely thought about such matters-- or at least if they did never spoke them openly. I think it remarkable that a lovely girl with such vital potential should be interested in the past of dead civilizations."

"Of course, not everything your Uncle Jeremiah believes based on real science;" interjects her father. "He tends to spend too much time in tombs of the dead and not enough attention tending to affairs of the living."

This remark more aimed at the fact that Jeremiah had two failed marriages and no children of his own. Hannah is still too young at the time to catch the full implication of this statement.

"In answer to your question: there is much accumulated evidence suggesting that the structure of the Great Pyramid predates a cataclysm, which reconfigured our planet. I think it no coincidence that structures of similar design exists on the other side of our globe bearing the same polyhedron shape and with corresponding mass. Nor is it alone in the archives of ancient architectures positioned on the earth astronomically aligned to planetary rotational harmonics relative to the fixed stars that fall well outside the parameters of conservative time tables. It is my belief that these aligned structures like capacitors on a circuit board prepared for an unquantifiable compatible energy release to complete the circuit."

"Then what happens?"

"The same thing that happened the first time, only next time it will be much worse. The minds responsible for creation of this technology are blind to the implication of design. Remember Hannah, there is nothing new under the sun. I believe completely that the riddle to destiny, a question already answered in forensics of the past."

Before Hannah can respond, her younger sister comes running into the room. Immediately, seriousness of the conversation ends. Nevertheless, she will continue to think for many years to come about the meaning in her uncle's theories. It is as though that night Hannah inspired to know more of what Jeremiah knows, and join his obsession to reassemble shattered pieces of a puzzle making the jumbled collage of past civilizations.

Hannah's younger sister, Rachel, always more like their mother, more on earth, and more practical. Physically the two sisters look very much alike growing up, the same color hair, the same eyes and skin tone. But in spirit very different. Rachel more bubbly, more of what a girl should be through gender-bias; whereas, Hannah has tendency to be too much analytical, always searching for clues of hidden meaning.

"You sometimes think too much like a boy." Rachel reprimands her often, as they get older. "There is so much more to life than books about science and lost kingdoms. Father thinks you spend too much time reading and not enough planning about future of a family."

"Can't you see, Rachel, how important history is to modern day scientific discovery and the future direction of humankind? Uncle Jeremiah has devoted his entire life to resurrect meaning to many things marvelous from the past. He believes every archeological discovery a gift or a warning to the future."

"Even father says that Uncle Jeremiah has lost his way through obstacle of his own brilliance. Why should you jeopardize the most important years in a woman's life, as well as your own professional reputation, pursuing theories that will never be proven? Surely you must admit that some of his ideas about pyramids and ancient gods a bit on the fringe."

"I am not saying that his every idea holds the same value of logic. But there is a lot of intriguing possibility to his observations. Don't worry little sister, I like my new job as a museum curator; nor do I intend to jeopardize it, not even for our beloved relative. But just between us, I promise that Uncle Jeremiah is not wrong about everything."

The years pass. Rachel gets married to a nice Jewish boy living in the suburbs, whose career is selling medical supplies to hospitals. Within the first few years they have two children, a boy and a girl, which is enough to satisfy their family aspirations. Then she and her husband begin attending a non-denominational church located in the suburbs of Long Beach. Not Jewish-- *but Christian--* something her father has particular difficulty accepting.

"Remember, Rachel, it was the Christians responsible for allowing what happened in Germany by closing their eyes to the calculated murder of millions. How could a religion based on a philosophy of love be conspirator to systematic genocide?"

"Not all Christians closed their eyes, and many were executed along with the Jews because of conviction in their hearts. True Christianity is not a religion of some collective institution, but a living testament of individual faith. As with Judaism, either God is alive, or an expression of dead custom. All this beside, father, Jesus was a Jew, as were all his apostles. To believe in Jesus Christ, as God's Messiah, does not make me any less Jewish."

"Then why would not Rabbis, who study the Torah daily, not come to the same conclusion? Are you saying that now you know more than thousands of years of teaching?"

"No father. What I am saying is that Messiah is prophesized by chosen men even before God first spoke to Abraham in a dream. Only because of religious obstinacy is Jesus not believed. But Mark and I have both been touched by the Holy Spirit, now knowing what we did not know before. But all this aside, I still love you and mother, as always I have loved. Only now my love constructed from a source more profound and unconditional."

Although neither parent is all that much religious in the traditional sense, attending Temple only on High Holidays, they choose to ostracize their daughter based on history of collective prejudice. It takes father and mother several months to get use to the idea that Rachel now attending a Christian fellowship. Upon realizing it more than just a passing fad, they accept her back, considering that part of her life of less importance than the absence of their charismatic favorite child.

As for Hannah, she dates a few men, even almost gets married once or twice, only not yet ready to compromise committed dedication to her career as rare antiquities curator at the Los Angeles County Museum of Art. Now approaching thirty-five, it begins to seem unlikely that she will follow in her sister's footsteps by submitting to the idea of family.

That is until one day while visiting Cairo in search of artifacts to be placed on permanent display at the museum. On this trip Hannah meets Jack Mateo, a brazen ex-Marine, who will also be instrumental to the greatest discovery of her career.

Jack Mateo has lived on and off the grid ever since taking his discharge from the military after a tour in Vietnam. He is --what may be termed in the world of antiquities-- a "*finder*". He seems to know everyone, and everyone seems to know him. He speaks the common language, understanding well the vernacular of horse-trading. Jack Mateo can be both a gentleman and a hardened negotiator, but also borders on being a scoundrel. Their first meeting goes badly, when Hannah introduced by a local colleague affiliated with the Egyptian Museum in Cairo.

"This is Jackie," he says taking Hannah firmly by the arm. "If you want anything, here is the man that can find it for you."

"The name is Jack-Mateo." He corrects without even a smile. "But it is true that I have a lot of good connections-- but for a price."

"Of course, the museum will gladly reimburse your efforts. But you must also remember that we are a respected society and strictly governed by international statues concerning antiquities."

Hannah's tone says more than her words. She has met men like this before. Those that only work for profit, willing to rob graves just for a morsel; nevertheless, she is willing to give him a chance based on the integrity of her contact here at the *Egyptian Museum* in the heart of *Tahrir Square*. This is not her first time in Egypt, nor is it the first time she has come face to face with a handsome *Smiling Jack*. After many years, Hannah has gained reputation as one of the best curators of antiquities-- *not because she is fluent in foreign languages or even because of sensitivity to other cultures*-- but because she has a good eye, knows well her history, and can be shrewd as any man when closing a deal.

"Not everyone in this land eats at a Sultan's table." Jack Mateo emphasizes, glancing sideways at the smaller man beside Hannah. "But that doesn't make them thieves and grave robbers. Most everyone in this country lives poor compared to western societies. To most here the land is sacred, their crops and their fields bountiful blessing during a good harvest, believing heritage of the past belongs to all in common."

"So Mr. Mateo your personal beliefs are that local bedlam populations qualified to determine survival of records that resurrect knowledge of the ancient past?"

"I believe that resurrection of the dead past a concept of future edification, but not at the expense of present value. What good is knowledge of the past if children of the present crowd under the table empty? History represents the suckled nativity from one's own land, not the private commodity of only an elite few."

He sounds so much like Uncle Jeremiah, Hannah thinks to herself. She also likes the intensity of his wintry green eyes and the strong appearance of his hands. But more than this, Hannah feels her body truly alive for the first time-- feels his attraction to her! And these only beginning reasons she will inevitably fall in love with Jack Mateo.

Two days later he leaves a message at the Windsor Hotel lobby for her to meet him for lunch at a nearby cafe. Both charmed and apprehensive, Hannah accepts the invitation.

"I have found something I think you and your museum will be interested in," he says during the course of their cuisine.

"How much do you want if I decide?"

"Twenty percent of the asking-- plus allow me to take you out on another date before going back to America."

She accompanies this man of rugged appeal on an hour and forty minute drive outside Cairo into desert ending at a small simple sun-baked brick home built on an Oasis. Like everywhere, the poorer inhabitants, a man, his wife, along with an eldest daughter express happiness for the rare opportunity to receive visitors. They offer their guest *Karkadeh*, a kind of tea made from dried hibiscus flowers, served with thin sugar wafers. Acting as translator Jack Mateo wastes no time, making it immediately clear for what reason he and his female companion have come. The patron of the household goes to an adjacent room and brings out something obviously heavier than it appears.

The unusual obelisk stands approximately three feet tall, tapering into a ziggurat, and with an irregular circumference of no more than twelve inches at the base. He places the unusual artifact on the floor beside the kitchen table. Several scars of hack marks appear along the hexagonal edges of the black exterior, evidence that someone in the past had attempted its destruction using dull instruments. Closer examination reveals an image carved middle of the structure with a triangular shaped crater gouged into left side of the face. Hannah recognizes the effigy immediately to be profile of the Ancient Egyptian God Osiris, missing his eye.

"Where did you find this?" Hannah questions excitedly.

The two women smile shyly, both surprised and pleased by the forthrightness of this woman from another culture. After a brief exchange with the farmer, Jack Mateo interprets that this relic has been a family heirloom for more than three generations, ever since his great ancestor found it buried in a crop field while plowing.

"Because of present need, the man is willing to sell this personal treasure to your museum for 2000 Egyptian Pounds." Jack concludes.

Immediate arrangements made and the artifact transferred to the Alexandria Port that very evening. The Egyptian government easily processes all the paperwork, allowing the North American museum to retain the enigmatic damaged artifact on terms considered an indefinite loan. Back in Los Angeles expert analysis of the unusual antiquity reveals that the missing eye not the result of damage, but for some reason intentionally designed this way. Even more curious is that within the recess is a nearly smooth plate of copper, parallel to another composed of nickel, inconsistent with the solid black basalt block used to sculpt the obelisk. Yet there are no detectable seams or faults to suggest that the source rock anything other than product of a natural phenomenon. Nevertheless, this would remain a mystery of much speculation.

Hannah decides to stay another week in Cairo to become better acquainted with the charming Jack Mateo. He is a man of average height, sandy hair, and eyes intensely green that have seen too many things he will never talk about. It cannot be said that Jack Mateo particularly handsome, nor is he physically unattractive. But the thing that most draws Hannah is a sense of emptiness in the man, which she knows instinctively her presence able to fill; and that he also revives within her being a dimension of meaning not felt before.

This beginning of a relationship quickly changes romantic. Jack Mateo confides that he grew up an only child, both his parents older by the time they married and conceived. He describes his childhood as being often lonely, wishing to have a brother or sister. A month after turning seventeen, he joined the Marine Corps and discovered a sense of belonging not felt before. But the worse of it, both Jack Mateo's parents tragically killed in an automobile accident a year later, so he volunteers for combat duty and ships-off to Nam. Upon returning he receives an honorable discharge and attends university on the GI Bill with a burning interest in the heavens. Only Jack Mateo is not the type to sit complacent behind a telescope looking at those stars only; his knowledge of the real world too great, his soul too restless to remain long in one place.

Hannah begins to better understand this Jack Mateo; and why a man of his intelligence and education would choose to live on the fringe of modern society. Even more meaningful, she starts to comprehend for the first time in her life what Rachel has been saying since many years.

Six months later Jack Mateo gives-up his Cairo apartment and moves to Santa Monica, California. After several weeks of intense courtship, he and Hannah consider the idea of marriage. Sister Rachel loves him immediately, happy that her older sibling finally engaged. She can tell Hannah's love not based on infatuation, as has been the case in times past. And for Rachel this all that's truly important. The fact Jack Mateo only half Jewish on side of his father, who married a Japanese woman after the Second World War, causes some early friction with Hannah's mother. But this soon passes because of his soft-spoken, yet strong manner. To the despair of both parents, it seems their two daughters determined to break every boundary of tradition.

Hannah's father is the first seduced by Jack Mateo's natural charm. Although Samuel never admits it, he always wanted a son, someone more like himself. He embraces Mark as an acceptable son-in-law, a good provider for his family, but never feels a deep bond of kinship. But this Jack Mateo more a man after his own heart-- a man he is proud to call his son! Even more surprising, Jeremiah also likes Jack right away, which is a relief, since her uncle rarely took easily to anyone.

Jack Mateo becomes everything Hannah desired to find in a man. She sees in his eyes, and feels within her own body, his mutual love and respect. Within the year, Jack Mateo relocates permanently to Southern California, where he starts a landscaping business to be near Hannah. With his university degree in Astronomy, he acquires a second night job at the Griffith Observatory, where he categorizes star charts.

Beginning of spring, they set a wedding date mostly because of pressure from Rachel and Hannah's mother. It is a simple non-traditional ceremony hosted in a tropical park surrounding a small lake near the *J. Paul Getty Museum,* thanks in part to special arrangements made because of Hannah's professional connections. It is an emotional gathering of family and friends, filled with photos and tears, as even Uncle Jeremiah's one eye changes glassy during the final vows. As predicted no one attended in support of the groom; therefore, Hannah's uncle fills-in as best man. At least now a family connection restored to Jack Mateo not known since a long time. This might have been the end of this story were it not for a later precipitation of events.

Hannah's father takes suddenly ill and dies quickly of an undiagnosed condition. Uncle Jeremiah attends the funeral, flying all the way from Istanbul, where he is intensely engaged in unearthing lost remnants of the Ottoman and Byzantine empires. Hannah has not seen or heard from her uncle since the wedding, and she remarks how much he has changed in just two years.

"Samuel was a good brother and a good family man." Her uncle says matter-of-factly. "He feared often that you might take too much after me and become consumed in work. Thankfully, he was only part right."

"I understand how easy it is to get lost. There is so much more in the past-- so much more to planet earth that remains a mystery. No wonder you chose the life you did Uncle Jeremiah. World history is greater than any one lifespan. The more I scratch the surface, the deeper I see."

"And it is even deeper still. Samuel placed much of his faith in science, without fully considering that science should be seen as a tool based on reasonable ideas of assumption. But models tell only some of the story. This fact your father did not wish to see... and deep down I understand why."

Jeremiah pauses, looks into the eyes of his niece. Such young eyes-- eyes meant to see so much more. As he has grown older, his deficiency of sight has become more pronounced, his one good eye bulging slightly like that of a vulture. But to Hannah it is the face of her uncle, the only brother of her now deceased father, gazing affectionately down at her, as always he did when she was still a child.

"Mother says it is because of what happened in Germany when you were children. That when the Fascist took control it terrified father more."

"It terrified us both to see our friends and neighbors begin to shun us as though we no longer belonged. It wasn't that much easier in America in the beginning. Sewn into many societies of this world is belief that Jews the cause of all evil, with anti-Semitism always lurking beneath the veneer, waiting for an excuse to surface. This fact was hardest for your father to accept. I later embraced a spiritual meaning and found faith. Lack of faith was always something Samuel struggled with. Many of our disagreements had more to do with phenomenon that science of modern society alone cannot explain or reconcile conclusively. But your father is not alone when it comes to the disconcerting idea that there is an invisible world; and that time and event only relative conditions. There are things impossible to quantify, so profound in meaning that it threatens many guarded premises of modern scientific theorem. The danger is not if such power exists. The greater existential threat is resurrection of such power, and placing it in the hands of limited comprehension blind to greater consequence."

Hannah truly marvels at her uncle's intellect. He is a genius in her mind, a man that has exceeded the sum of his learned knowledge of accepted fact. Her adoration, no longer that of a little girl scurrying in the shadows at his feet; rather it is respect built on a foundation of comprehension and shared ideology. Without needing to say it, she knows exactly what he is talking about.

"Then why have you devoted so much of your life to discovering sources of past technology, while at the same time being aware of the inherent dangers once you find it."

"Because I know and have known since a very long time the minds instrumental in creation of technologies did so in an attempt to change thermodynamic process. This is an evil directive guaranteeing annihilation of all matter and energy in this universe of temporal design. My quest is not to resurrect it, Hannah, but to keep it out of hands of an unwise generation for as long as possible."

"So you believe mankind should remain ignorant and that knowledge inside Pandora's Box better left sealed?"

"That is your father talking," Jeremiah says smiling. "My older brother was wise about a lot of things. He was wise to have a family and to place the needs of that family first. Yes, I have come to realization that there are things better left in the dark. I am glad, Hannah, that you, as a woman, possess qualities I lack as a man."

A moment of respectful silence punctuates the conversation, saying more than words able to express.

"I acquired something for the museum a few years back I think you might find interesting." Hannah remarks cheerfully. "We are trying to categorize it as part of an Egyptian Exhibit opening this fall."

"What, another mummy?"

"It is like nothing I have ever seen. A ziggurat composed of black basalt apparently chiseled from a single rock. This strange obelisk depicts the Egyptian god Osiris with a deep cavity where the eye should be. We plan to perhaps name it *'The Blind Osiris'.*"

"I must see this Blind Osiris before I leave. My return flight to Turkey is in less than twenty hours. I will meet you tomorrow noon at the museum."

This was more of a demand than request. Hannah had not planned to return to the office so soon after the funeral. At the same time she is excited to share her unique find with the one person that will most surely understand and appreciate it. But more it is her hope that her uncle's experience might shed some context to the piece for the purpose of categorization.

The next day Jeremiah arrives punctually. He only grunts approvingly at the extensive collection gathered through the years. Upon coming to the obelisk in the restoration room, he freezes in his tracks, carefully studying every detail.

"I would like to introduce our Blind Osiris." Hannah says, sounding apologetic. "We can't find another like it on record, and there is a great deal of speculation about its chronology and meaning."

"I'm sure there is Hannah," he says, removing his wire-rimmed glasses.

He reaches into his coat pocket and retrieves a small flashlight. Shining a beam into the cavity, his one good eye peers into the well like a Cyclops searching diligently for some specific detail.

"Do you see something Uncle Jeremiah?" Hannah enquires after several moments of silence.

"And you are the one that discovered this artifact?"

"Actually it was Jack Mateo, who first heard about its existence while living in Egypt. But I am essentially the one to bring it here. Why, do you recognize something about it?"

"I always knew it-- *felt it in my gut!* At last things begin to make sense. Rachel is the soul; but you, Hannah, the spirit. Now I am convinced of preparation in everything. I often wondered why you? Why would God choose a woman to continue this most important investigation? Now I think I know. If this ziggurat obelisk is what I think, then it represents something of critical meaning going back before construction of the Babylon Tower."

Never has she seen her uncle this giddy about anything. It is as though this Blind Osiris holds answers to the quest of a lifetime.

"I feel certain I have in my possession an important part to this puzzle. At present it is imperative that I return to Istanbul. We are at an important stage excavating a hippodrome during the time of Constantinople, but should be wrapping things up at end of this year. After that I will come back here. There is something in my New Jersey apartment that may open possibilities of knowledge so tempting as to tempt even me. If this is what I think it is, then it represents a master key to unlock ancient powers designed within the pyramids. Now I am certain you are the one sent by God to help guide me in wisdom."

"What are you talking about Uncle Jeremiah? What can I possibly do to help you?"

"Hannah, there exist powers incomprehensible to mortal reason. Forces so great and seductive, that even time and space becomes compressed into the singularity of a thought. As a man, I may not be strong enough; but as a woman, I think you able to see things more organic, and less through the rational of ego. From the beginning, I knew there was a reason why God chose you to follow in the steps of my driven curiosity."

"I still do not understand what all this has to do with the obelisk."

"I believe there to be a complex web of interconnected matrixes intelligently designed into certain ancient structures found today upon the earth. These architectures are not just old, but originate from a civilization altogether different-- *a time before the flood of Noah*! They have survived not by accident, but for a purpose, existing as cosmic topographical markers. Their purpose is much like our present-day computer chips, but on a much larger scale, capable of transforming channeled energy streams from a source of mass energy not yet defined through present observation of entropic condition. Once that power source reactivated, a host of dormant machines will turn on, escalating to the end of everything. As stated by the Prophet Isaiah: *'All the stars will be dissolved and the heavens rolled up like a scroll'*."

"You really start to frighten me."

Hannah has never seen her uncle like this. Now he truly was acting like the mad scientist always her father predicted. Yet, she knows also that he is not mad.

"Can't you see? The original architects of this technology wanted to change entropic destiny-- to rewrite the code of life to make themselves eternal!"

"Who wanted to rewrite this code you refer to and for what reason? Wouldn't a world without death and corruption be better? "

"Would it really, Hannah, be better? Imagine this world as we experience it without change. Things are born and die for a reason. Our souls are created to live, not die to the end of oblivion. I have often been referred to as a crack pot to believe in what I am about to tell you. Even my own brother thought it. I believe in Bible passages that make inference to a race of super beings referred to as the *Nephilim*. These mortal offspring of fallen angels, mixed with the *DNA* of humankind, are described with greater detail in the *Book of Enoch*. Their knowledge of mechanical process far greater than present comprehension, which will make them seem to our technologically seduced society as gods. Their fathers are the gods of legend found throughout world history. Only these gods have no future. To them time is a firefly existence doomed to eventual extinction. The limit of their truth is the lie they want mankind to believe: *that the knowledge of change a thing to be feared.* It is still the same lie today, as told to Adam and Eve in the garden."

"I agree that finite existence as we presently experience would be impractical. Still, I think modern man has far outgrown the awe of a better fire stick and fairytale stories."

"But what if that fire stick is capable of changing laws of subatomic process. In other words, what if they are able to change our notion of perceived reality?"

"So who are these *Nephilim* really, and what makes you think they can be resurrected after all this time?"

"Because, Hannah, they have never left. To them time is not a constant of quantum value, but dimensional prison. Since they are the direct offspring of a fallen principality, once released they will try again as before. Yet, they still do not see the fatal flaw in their calculations."

"What flaw Uncle Jeremiah?"

"Entropy is the gift of something better, if only one might see the true meaning. Even fairytales contain a source of fact at the core if one might dare to believe with the heart. There is something else, Hannah. I also have a letter I believe to be written by the prophet Joseph from when he is an old man living in Egypt. Joseph's life has always been of special interest to me. A man betrayed to death by his brothers, yet found peace with God, becoming instrument to deliver those same men in accordance to a destiny of greater design."

Hannah feels a sudden jolt of apprehension, never felt before. It will be much later by the time she fully understands the true depth of this conversation. She and

her uncle affectionately hug goodbye and agree to see
each other again in a few months. Only this will be the last
time she will see her Uncle Jeremiah alive.

Several weeks later Hannah's mother receives news
that their uncle dead as result of an unforeseen work
accident. Like his brother, he dies suddenly and without
explanation, leaving Hannah and Rachel devastated. It is
like losing father all over again-- and so soon!

Arrangements are made to have the body flown directly
to LAX so that the two brothers might be buried together in
accordance to their wishes. Hannah and Rachel then fly to
New Jersey to settle their uncle's affairs. Mother would
have gone, only she could not see the point. Everyone
she knew alive or dead now in California, and there was
nothing for her on the east coast. So it is decided that her
two daughters make the journey on their own.

The apartment is much smaller than anticipated. Their
uncle had lived here for the past 30 years, or at least it was
his home base when he was not off somewhere in the
world digging up graves. Every shelf, every tabletop,
nearly every wall in the small three-room dwelling, holds a
relic from somewhere in the world representing past and
present history. To Hannah it is much like entering a
closet in the museum where she works. Stacked in each
dusty corner and along the walls are moldering remnants
of past dynasties awaiting imaginative restoration.

"Look at this Hannah, something addressed to you,"
Rachel says, handing her a small burlap bundle tied with
string, along with a yellowed envelope bearing her name.

Inside the envelope is a letter obviously written many
years prior, chilling reminder that Jeremiah gone, and now
as much part of history as everything else here.

*"I remember so many years ago a young girl asked me
the most bravely profound question ever asked by anyone
before. She wanted to know meaning of the pyramids and*

their origin. Even then I believed there something more to their design than just elaborate burial chambers, but could provide no convincing answer as to the why. Now I know more, but still not enough. Today that girl is a grown woman, and someone I now respect as a colleague of equal status. I leave here mystery of a scroll painfully translated, along with an artifact of curious design. I believe the scroll to be a record made by Joseph of Egypt, concerning a dream he had in later life. This before another Pharaoh sits upon the throne of the kingdom, which did not remember this remarkable man or his God. All before the Israelites made slaves to serve a principality turned decadent. This questionable piece of a greater puzzle is a polyhedron shaft composed mostly of black basalt depicting an eye and wrapped in a scroll written in ancient Hebrew. Both sealed in a coffin and buried in one of the catacombs west of the Great Pyramid outside Gaza. On the opposite end of this precisely hewn instrument are embedded copper and nickel nodules, which I believe to be a key to something referenced in Joseph's text. For the past twenty-five years I have been looking for the lock this key fits. If it is what I think, then it could very well rewrite history as we know it. I leave this evidence in your curious hands, Hannah. It is my hope you will be the one to discover the meaning that this key unlocks and be wise enough to know what to do with it."

Wrapped within the burlap bundle is a small sarcophagus measuring six inches long and three inches in circumference stamped by symbol of a scarab carved into the face. It is sealed and locked. The means to open it not found, although searched for diligently.

"I am not certain, Rachel, but if this is what I think it is, then it makes Uncle Jeremiah right about everything!"

"What do you mean, Hannah?"

Hannah begins to relay her last meeting with their uncle, describing his level of excitement that day only a few months earlier upon examination of the obelisk at the museum.

"He believed he had in his possession a key that could unlock something very important, and perhaps even dangerous to the future of humankind. I think this might be the thing he was referring to."

"I feel there could be something evil inside," Rachel says, apprehensively taking her sister's hand. "We should pray, and I will ask my church to pray about it when we arrive back home."

Not wishing to damage the historical significance of the artifact, Hannah determines to wait until she is back in Los Angeles before any further attempts to open the sarcophagus. Some of their uncle's things they would take back as museum donations. The rest Hannah and her sister give to Good Will.

After settlement of all her uncle's worldly affairs, Hannah shares with Jack the amazing interest of her find. Having had experience with similar obstructions, he feels confident in his skill to pick the lock without damage. Several moments later, the lid pops open. Inside is an unusual triangularly shaped instrument made of black basalt, with emblem of an eye on face of one end, and a copper and nickel module on the end opposite. With it is an original scroll written in Hebrew, along with a translation carefully made by Uncle Jeremiah.

I, Joseph, had a dream in latter days of Egypt. A burning pillar appears in heaven surrounded by five eyes with different magnitudes and proportions. These eyes set in a pattern of divine purpose. Then one eye glows brighter than all the rest. From this eye great power erupts, causing all the other eyes to shake. From beyond the fifth eye appears another eye that travels toward the

center passing between two sister-eyes momentarily close.
Both eyes seem to blink, changed less glorious than
before. The new eye after it has passed between the
sister eyes becomes the sixth according to its number, and
moves into a pattern around the center, taking place as a
new second eye after the first. Then one of the sister
eyes, now third from the center, gives birth to a smaller eye
that circles near like a child suckling its mother, following a
pattern witnessed now in the night sky. In a time divided
by time all eyes fade, until only darkness prevails.

　　After this dream I awake shaken by the vision, yet no
interpretation given. I ask the Egyptian magicians and
astrologers if they had ever heard of such things as seen
in my dream, but all refuse to give answer. Unable to
sleep I search alone through rooms of one of the older
temples. I find in a chamber an unusual column erected
upon a pedestal bearing the image of one of the Egyptian
gods named Osiris with a deep pyramid recess where the
eye should have been. Next to it is a small casket with a
stone shaft inside having the same shape as the recess.
Carved upon its face is insignia of the missing eye.
Feeling compelled by reason, I remove the eye and insert
this shaft into the cavity. A spark travels through my hand
and along my arm. The eye, now the eye of Osiris, begins
to glow, filling the chamber with shining presence of many
other eyes. My dream reappears in the waking moment.
Then I, Joseph, understand the interpretation thereof. This
is the power that destroyed the world that was before days
of the Great Drowning, a force meant to remain dormant
for now. This is also reason to why the Egyptians refused
my inquiries. They know that for now the knowledge of this
harnessed destruction must remain hidden. Therefore, I
Joseph, Chief Steward of the Kings House, and Servant to
the Most High God, do seal record of this heavenly event
with warning that the day its power resurrected will herald
an end of days. It is by mortal decree that the eye of Osiris

remain separated and buried along with this scroll far removed from knowledge of men, until the time of restoration, when angels shall fight the final great battle."

Avoiding further conversation, Hannah grabs Jack Mateo by the arm and together they rush over to the Museum taking rush-traffic congested Wilshire Boulevard. Although the institution closed to visitors, Hannah has a keycard granting special access as Head Curator. Once inside they go to the storage room containing inventory of future exhibits. Here the Blind Osiris stands mounted on a pedestal in the center. Without explanation, she removes the shaft containing the eye with the nickel and copper modules facing down. It is a perfect fit. Upon touching the bottom of the well, a mild electrical shock travels up and along her arm; then the eye recesses slightly, begins glowing.

Jack pulls his wife protectively close and steps back. Suddenly, an array of holographic lights shoot out of the obelisk, creating a map of planets in the air that begin moving according to a designed trajectory around a large body projecting from center of Osiris' one eye.

"Hannah, this is a map closely resembling our inner Solar System," Jack affirms in amazement. "The one closes is Mercury, and those two bodies near the center are the Earth and Mars. The two larger ones at farthest distant I am quite certain are Saturn and Jupiter. The eye of Osiris is our sun marking the center. Only there is one planet missing."

As the projection continues, another beam shoots out from the center eye causing a satellite planetoid to move out of orbit and away from one of the larger planets. This rogue traveler passes between the Earth and Mars at their closest perigee. Then all the planets begin wobbling. The planet Jack describes as the Earth expels a mass that becomes a smaller orbiting body. The rogue planetoid continues on a trajectory toward the center, finally settling into an orbital path between the Earth and Mercury.

"I know what this is, Hannah!" Jack exclaims. "A highly contested theory in Cosmology is a stellar cataclysm termed the *Theia Event*. It supposes that in the distant past a rogue satellite somehow escaped orbit from one of the gas giants, and either collided with, or swiped the Earth, causing a change in mass, thus creating the lunar orbital body of Earth's Moon. More exaggerated models suggest the planet Venus is actually *Theia*, a giant rogue moon, most likely from Jupiter, either escaped or was forced out of orbit, causing it to pass between Earth and Mars at their closest proximity. According to the theory this would have created a shearing effect, ripping atmosphere and mass debris from both planets, with our lunar body as an aftermath. This would explain the discrepancy why the Earth's molten core larger than it should be for a planet its size, and why Mars left with only a limited atmosphere. This model creation further provides explanation of why Venus is the only planet in the observable solar system with a counter rotation. This stellar recreation represents the greatest discovery ever made!"

"No, it's not. It is the prophesized fulfillment of my uncle's greatest fear. Once this Pandora secret escapes, it will mean the end of life as we know it."

"What are you talking about, Hannah? This is the answer to questions old as time! It proves that the *Theia Event* happened, and that at least in part your uncle was right about the past containing secrets of ancient lost civilizations."

"Or it could also mean the end of time. My father was right to submit to a life more simple. He witnessed firsthand how potentially dark human nature could be and realized nothing he might do to change it. He foresaw the ultimate carnage promised by technological warfare. Because of advances achieved by the Nazi war machine, the world accelerated in creating even greater weapons of mass destruction. He believed that once an armament conceived, it will be used, controlled nuclear fission only the first step into grave of annihilation. Therefore, father devoted his life to the needs of his family instead of trying to change the world. Now I realize this beginning and end of true wisdom. Uncle Jeremiah always the dreamer, believing evil in the world, yet hoping in a better future through mortal reason. But Jeremiah wrong to think father lacked faith. It is just that his faith of a different interpretation. So he made family his life, silent in the face of events beyond his control, submitting to responsibility and devotion to challenges within context of the present. I once judged him as a man lacking curiosity, interested only in the mundane. Now realize I was wrong. Uncle Jeremiah always able to see more the mechanics of true evil, but also in error to believe father lacked faith. It is just that his faith of a different sort."

"Hannah, we can't turn our backs on knowledge this important. Even your father would agree--"

"No Jack Mateo-- we must return this eye of Osiris back into the obscurity of history from where it came."

"What do you mean return it," Jack says, glaring at his wife in agitation. "This is the most important clue to unlocking mystery of the ancient past ever discovered. *And we-- no-- not we-- you discovered it!*"

"That is exactly the reason we need to keep it just between us. Don't you see that this is what once destroyed the earth? My Uncle Jeremiah was not only a scientist, but a Biblical scholar, who also studied to be a Rabbi. His obsession not based on just reviving those technologies that existed before the cataclysm described in the *Book of Genesis*, but about the ones really responsible for that level of destruction. He believed with certainty that ancient pyramids and structures like it are immense dormant energy conduits waiting for the one key to unlock the mystery of their design. *This eye is that key*!"

"The key made to open what Hannah, and whose return?"

"Return of the *Nephilim*, children of fallen angels, the ones responsible for the cataclysm, which destroyed earth in the past." Hannah says taking her husband's hand and looking steadfast into his wondrous green eyes.

"You realize how that sounds, Hannah."

"I know Jack Mateo. And only just now tonight do I believe it all to be true. In later years, my Uncle Jeremiah began to realize that existence of the entire universe analogist to a caterpillar changing into a butterfly. He understood that as wondrous the present unfolding magnitude of existence, this only transitional to something better and incomprehensible. Why even the pod of a seed planted and made to disintegrate so that an invisible germ encoded within takes root. It is all about resurrection of a new code. He once told me and my sister, *'God is the immeasurable measure of eternal life, not the calculated fear of death. There is a time to all things under heaven that not even the angels know. But nothing really dies, only changes. Entropy is not the curse of fear, but evidence of greater promise'*."

"I liked your Uncle Jeremiah-- more than liked-- I respected him. But how can anyone know the real meaning of the past or what's in store for the future?"

"He knew. This is what my Uncle Jeremiah was saying when last we spoke. He feared he might not be strong enough, but believed me capable of a different choice. Can't you see that the world is not ready to know this kind of power-- if ever it will be? The completed obelisk is only part of a much grander agenda. Just as the shaft containing Osiris' eye a key to switch on this device, I think this reassembled obelisk also a key. A key made for a specific socket prepared in one of the larger pyramids.

Once inserted, it will reanimate some dormant potential. My uncle believed that harbored within the alignment of these structures, along with other locations marked by ancient *geoglyph* constructions upon the earth and beyond, are embedded energy conduits designed to initialize a chain reaction. In his heart, Jeremiah wished to warn mankind of imminent danger, not hasten its demise."

"But Hannah those are stories based on myth and legend no one can prove. Knowledge like this will help us harness the power of the universe and reach to the stars. It could also be answer to saving our planet!"

"Save it for whom, Jack Mateo? Can't you see that only cold emptiness of space exists beyond? My uncle did not believe those writings to be myth, nor do I believe it-- nor did the Egyptians that carefully preserved the machinery of this technological potential. They were aware that what happened in the past remains in preparation for a future end. If we allow resurrection of this knowledge, then we will be the ones responsible. Even the prophet Joseph recognized the evil minds that imagined this device into existence. He understood that it must remain hidden from the consciousness of men, until it can be hidden no longer. This is the thing the Nazi *SS* were looking for; the reason they did so judiciously scour the earth in search of occult artifacts. Those same minds are still present today. Minds darkened by hate and prejudice. The rise of demigods that will once again focus greatest attention against the Jews, just because Jews represent an abiding testament to a world of divided principalities of a living God not conceived according to elemental pattern. My Uncle Jeremiah knew this. In my heart I now know it too. We must make the same choice he would have wanted to make. This is what my uncle was saying the last time I saw him. Instinctively, he felt that because I am a woman and daughter of his more grounded brother, I would be capable of making the wiser decision."

Placing Jack's hand on her abdomen, she begins stroking his crinkled brow. Immediately his face brightens upon realizing the meaning. The miracle of a new life had come at last to the isolated emptiness of his wilderness existence. After many dark years and the scars left by war, there is future hope, a seed planted that has finally taken root. This moment he believes Hannah right. He believes that things past ought to remain dead and better forgotten. Pulling his wife against his chest, he kisses her, believing as he has not believed before.

It is a particularly hot desert afternoon six months later when a rental jeep arrives at the farmer's Oasis home nearly two hours into no man's land outside Cairo. The American couple stands sheepishly at the door holding something wrapped in burlap. Inviting these familiar faces inside, the farmer explains that the daughter has since been married off, leaving only him and his wife. After a few pleasantries, Jack Mateo removes wrappings of the burlap to unveil a small locked oblong coffin carved into likeness of a scarab.

"We will give you $1000 American dollars to take this and bury it in the desert where no one will find it. Only you must know the place and swear an oath never to tell another soul."

Both the farmer and his wife readily agree. They are both old now. With a thousand U.S. dollars they could move closer to a city, where food and medical attention more readily available. For them the scarab coffin is just another relic from an ancient past they know little about. It is just another dead artifact buried in the sand of their country for some future treasure hunter to find. Whereas, the thousand dollars theirs to spend as they please. Why should they care about the reason given?

Hannah and Jack Mateo return to California, where three months later she bears their first child naming her Proserpina. There would be many additions to the new Egyptian exhibit, but none as enigmatic as the Blind Osiris. Only Hannah, and her husband certain of its grander potential. Only they know that somewhere is a key awaiting future discovery that will one day unleash a harbinger of mass destruction as the world of constructed history has never experienced before.

Jack Mateo will think often about the grand power contained in the blind obelisk in the Egyptian section at the Los Angeles County Museum of Art. In part he is glad never to know where the eye of Osiris buried. Still when he peers through the lens of his one eyed telescope into immensity of a night sky, another part cannot help but marvel at the minds capable of changing course of planets. Then again maybe it is marvel of the heavens most marvelous, if only one might truly see and appreciate the clockwork design of their creation. With this he thinks about his wife and daughter, made content by vision of present bounty. His hope in tomorrow restored.

9

Sahra Moon Over Kahnawake

There is within eclipse of light and shadow a disco bar named Chiron's Gate located at a boulevard intersection where two Saints meet. Locals call the top floor of this citadel the Ziggurat, a place on a hill ascending above old and new Montreal. Here patrons come to dance, to get high, and just to forget.

Also many stories here; a place written with many endings. For some it is beginning of a new page where they emerge angels of light. Others with souls less innocent coiled in tentacles of dark imaginations. There are demons here, apostles, and prophets, too. Many lost, and some sent on special missions.

To enter one must cross beneath an arch with stained-glass windows, up two flights of stairs along a twisted corridor, and pass the nameless bouncer at the entrance known only as the *'Gatekeeper'*. He is an ogre with stone cold eyes and a mouth that never smiles. Rumor is that once he was a famous boxer before killing a man with his bare hands defending a patron street hooker. They say after he did his time that here the only place would hire him. Chiron's Gate knows its own and receives its own.

The beating heart of Chiron's Gate is a dimly-lit wooden dance floor that becomes a stage when there is a show. Outsiders call it *The Queen's Ramp*, a derogatory term meant to cast shadow of humiliation on the performers. Their candor short lived once the spectacle begins. Here nightshades blossom glamorous in hot flare of a spotlight. They are the true entourage that makes this Ziggurat famous. It is by magic of stage light and makeup illusion of stardom created, transforming dream into reality and reality fading into dream.

Once the lights dim, Black Misty steps from behind a curtain painted with florescent moon and stars and begins to sing, accompanied by chorus of birds on each extended arm. Black Misty is more than six feet tall in heels; and according to legend once played with the Harlem Globe Trotters before becoming a drag performer.

Next is beautiful Mercedes, who is as near to passing for a real girl as any you pass on the streets. She sings the hit songs of Celine Dion with flawless imitation, possessing elegant poise of a true performer. More than just her beauty, the audience falls in love with Mercedes' passion. And this is how she will always be remembered.

The most dynamic and energetic of the three is one named Dyanna, who immediately animates into a twirling Dervish, spinning around and around the stage. Her long dress opens into centrifuge of a turbine preparing to take flight, with bright flashing eyes and shoes that sparkle as fire. Hysterical applaud at the end, as all agree that there is no one able to match the raw energy released by Dyanna.

There are other performers as well, depending on the night. But I choose these three because of the particular tragedy of their lives. Dyanna ends up murdered, her naked body dumped under the overpass of Jacque Cartier Bridge by unknown assailants. Beautiful Mercedes will eventually meet someone, who promises to love her for the real woman she could be. A month after her surgery, he runs off with another Trans, saying only that he now realizes why he desired her in the first place. They find Mercedes a week later dead from an overdose of pain medication and a suicide note that simply reads: *"Now I know the heartbreak in being a woman."* Misty will eventually go blind from genetic macular degeneration, and just disappears. These are not the only souls sacrificed here. Only this is not their story, at least not now.

They say Johnny, a fat Greek that serves drinks from behind the mirrored reflection of a foursquare bar, owns the place. Of course this is a myth. Nevertheless, Johnny mixes the best Mai Tai and Whiskey Sours in town, with a cultivated way to make everyone he serves feel deserving. Chiron's Gate is the only place he has ever felt home; and here will remain epitaph to his memory.

There is the beautiful waitress named Jezebel, who is a real woman, whose day job includes exotic dancing in the topless bar downstairs. In this lair she could be anyone and have anyone, but prefers to remain independent. She will also be one of the few that eventually escapes on her own terms.

Faces come and faces go, except for the regulars that hangout here particularly on Saturday nights because they have nowhere else. I can tell you about some of these, but not all. Others know more, only most of them silenced by another kind of addition. Suffice it to say that Chiron's Gate holds many deep secrets, some more tragic than others. There are stories of demons and those possessed by them. And there are those stories made of dreams in a fairy tale complete with proud Princes and lovely Princesses. Also dragons here, armed with fangs and with deadly stings in their tails.

In one corner teeters Humpty Dumpty Serge propped against a wall, always swaying hypnotically back and forth. Everyone thinks he will fall and break, but he never does. No one would guess he is only half a man. Serge lost both his legs as a young boy while attempting to catch a train, except he slipped and got caught under the wheels. Wonder he did not bleed to death, except for the quick thinking of the *Boss Conductor*, who heard the young boy's screams from inside the Caboose. Now Serge drives the topless dancers that work downstairs to and from work in his limousine car. He speaks pleasantly and always smiling good-humoredly, completely bald and with clear blue eyes that twinkle in the flashing lights. Always there is a place in those eyes where he relives again and again the nightmare, the screams and the shock of a child condemned to walk the rest of life on wooden stilts.

George is best friend to Serge. George has a certain reputation here. *"George of the jungle- George the Terrible-- Good George-- bad George-- poor George"*-- and at the end it is always just George. To truly describe him is to try and describe a past living era. Although he is present in body, his mind always somewhere else far away and long ago, his eyes always glossed over by a hit of cocaine. If George could have fulfilled any one wish, it would be to return to the bygone days of the drug culture of the '60's. Not that he was really happier then, only he believed he was happy. This is both his torment and his relief— a self-made illusion to keep him always blind to the fact that he was never a good husband to his divorced wife or a good father to his only son. He once worked as a Library Technician for a prominent university, until he got caught with his hand in the coffee jar to feed his drug habit. He knows all the girls, and the girls know him. Of course, they are not all girls, which is what makes Chiron's Gate so special. George will end up spending the rest of his life in prison for accidentally killing his new drunken girlfriend he met while at rehab. One hangover morning he just loses control and slaps her over the balcony of their eighth floor apartment during a domestic argument.

"It was bad George," he declares always in the third person when he does something wrong. "George would never do that! George is a good person... *George could never do anything so terrible!*"

Tammy and Tiffani are as different as Mutt and Jeff, and also just as inseparable. Tiffani, once one of the beautiful people of this world, traveled between continents providing sexual entertainment to bored wealthy barons and kings as a talented female impersonator. In time Tiffani changed, tarnished by drugs and by lies of men. Originally from Uruguay, South America, disowned by family upon discovery their only son a Transvestite. Looking at pictures of Tiffani at her peak, she once made a beautiful cosmopolitan woman, tall, with chiseled high cheekbones, and lovely skin. Tiffani attributes the smoothness of the skin to a concentrated homemade lye treatment applied when only fifteen that could just as easily have made the child a monster. But what changed Tiffani most is when she had a fight with her unfaithful intoxicated gay boyfriend and jumped out the window from their second story Quebec City apartment, breaking her back. Tiffani's back healed in time, but not the spirit. When Tiffani is not out in the world with Tami, and is at home alone, she goes by Hector, her given birth name. She says that her alter ego able to protect against weakness of many temptations. There are few that wish to mess with Hector. And those who dare discover the demon of anger locked inside formidable. Tiffani will eventually die alone from AIDS, discovered in a praying position at the foot of her bed, and is buried nameless in a pauper's grave.

Tami is one of a kind, chubby and small, who proudly proclaims to be a *"street whore"*, whose professional hobby is to walk the avenues near her downtown apartment picking up tricks. Tami has an unusual bone deformation on the crown of a nearly bald head that anchors a cheap wig made of polyester. Often Tami dresses as a school girl, sometimes as an all out slut, concealed under a long overcoat in case a cop passes by. It is truly amazing how successful Tami is with a list of regulars and newcomers, too many invited home. The worst part of it is that Tami has a misogynistic hatred of women, but hates men even more. Tami claims to have learned from the best, following the footsteps of a streetwise prostitute mother providing to her only child little affection and even less protection against her predatory clients. Predictably, Tami is found one morning by the building superintendent because of a foul odor coming from the apartment. Tami had been dead for three days, naked, and with a towel tied around the neck, a reenactment of erotic pleasure depicted in a book of sadism written by *Marquis De Sade*.

The one they call the Pharmacist is really a breathing dragon inside lair of Chiron's Gate. He is a big time drug dealer of the Italian Mafia-- *or so they say*. He is always well-dressed, projecting worldly sophistication, and as song of the Rolling Stones goes: *"a man of wealth and taste."* No one is sure what he might have done in the past to climb up the mob ladder. There is one who has seen the real face of the Pharmacist and lived. Only she is certain of his true nature, a beast lurking in the shadows at the edge of city lights. And it is her story we will get to soon enough.

I should mention that there is one other within Chiron's Gate that does not altogether belong. On any given weekend you will find on the stage floor between shows, one they know only as the Dancing Girl. She comes and goes like a slither born of shadow. None see her really, and those that do remark how mostly she keeps to herself. She dances as a spirit in their minds, made free through music, seen as a reflection only, glimpsed in flash of light. Nothing they have she wants, not even gifts of the Pharmacist.

This could easily be her story from the beginning. Only somewhere in the middle is the best place to start. Let us just say that this Ziggurat has another kind of soul when this Dancing Girl present.

Sahra Moon, the Indian woman, wanders in from the street drunk. Always she comes in drunk, except this night she is more drunk than usual.

"I once was prettier than her!" She cries jealously, nearly falling at the feet of the Dancing Girl, their eyes meeting in passing reflection.

The Dancing Girl turns and twirls away just out of reach. She has seen this kind of suffering before, knowing that all pains must run course in time.

"At least I'm a real girl– *a real Indian girl!*" Cries Sahra again so that all might hear and be convinced.

Sahra Moon sways as though she might pass out; then stumbles off the stage, the heel of one silver slipper sliding on the last step, causing her to nearly fall. She appears instantly as a Gazelle spooked into flight, with long slender legs kicking under a tight florescent blue miniskirt, and with loose flowing auburn dyed hair swirling around a painted face marked by bloodshot eyes.

"Hello pretty baby, long time! How have you been?" The Pharmacist says subtly slithering to her aid.

Sahra Moon shrinks away from this man's familiar touch. He at least she recognizes. She knows who he is and what he is! Sahra once free-based with the Pharmacist for three days in a cheap motel room. On the third day he enquires if she wants to see what he truly is. The lights inside the room dim of their own accord and he transforms, becoming visage of a scavenger animal with eyes tormented and hungry.

"Now do you know me?"

"Yes," she replies weakly and begins praying silently in the name of Jesus, as once instructed by her religious aunt when all hope lost.

He then changes back into a man glorified by blindness of his own delusion. Sahra later escapes into the night, but will never again sleep the same. She knows that what she saw not just the hallucination of a drug trip. She has witnessed the beast of man and knows herself also snared in the same evil menagerie.

"No, Dan honey-- I got something to do tonight-- but maybe another time."

She has learned by now to always keep the door cracked open; but at least this night Sahra determines in herself to resist temptation of the devil.

The Pharmacist only winks. He is assured that sooner or later she will come back for a taste of sugar in his pocket-- *because they always do.* Sahra Moon manages to make it down the stairs and out to the sidewalk where incandescent city lights and the hungry night restores her beautiful again. At least here she is seen as a reigning queen of the night by those subject to her passing.

"Hey I know you," slurs a shadow from the dark alley beside Chiron's Gate.

"Forget it!" Sahra snarls cattily.

"Don't be like that! Here, take a swig from Snake's bottle."

The shadow changes to a man clutching a brown paper bag. The man and the bottle Sahra knows how to control. It is after all Saturday night-- *and Sahra Moon has a fire to quench!* Minutes later, she dazedly stumbles out of the dark passageway feeling the loss of something, only she cannot remember what. She hears her name mumbled, followed by angry smash of a bottle. Familiar sounds heard before. Always it is the same.

Sahra would have taken a cab and gone home, except she has no money. She is now prisoner of the city, trapped in a maze of lights, screaming traffic horns, and ghost of passing pedestrians. Deep down Sahra would have liked to be any one of them-- *anyone except a drunken Indian street whore!* In sudden panic, she seeks the familiar warmth of the *Come Back Inn,* a dingy little beer bar across the way with a *Peep Show* in the back.

"If it's not Sahra Moon, come have a drink with your friend, Dani."

Dani, a tall portly blonde American, has lived in Montreal ever since the Reagan years. She once loved her native country, but hates what it has become. She crossed the border to escape what she termed *'Capitalist Injustice'.* Dani was once a man and a highly paid Air Traffic Controller, until Regan's back to work legislation. After so many disappointments, she just never went back. Still, when a jet passes overhead, Dani looks up and sighs longingly.

"I'm broke," complains Sahra licking her lips.

"Of course you are Doll. Lou, give Sahra a *Boiler Maker* on my tab."

The bartender responds with a grunt of disapproval. He knows Sahra Moon all too well. Knows that a little beer made her happy, and too much whiskey possesses her, bringing out a wild Indian spirit. He can tell by her eyes that Sahra Moon has already had whiskey tonight and wanting more. However, Dani was a regular, so he sets up a jigger of his cheapest whiskey, then slides across the bar a bottle of beer with an empty glass, certain that Sahra will altogether ignore the glass. Lou makes it a point to study the habits of his regular clients. He knows that neither Dani nor Sahra know difference between good whiskey and cheap; or even care as long as it deadens the pain inside. As predicted, Sahra gulps down the shot, chased by a half bottle of beer.

"Thanks Dani," she breathes finishing the beer and verbosely slamming the empty bottle on the bar. "I really needed that!"

"Don't we all hugs," Dani sighs gazing emptily into her own glass.

Dani has known Sahra Moon through many years, remembered when she was still young and innocent, a beautiful girl with a voice as soft as April rain. Sahra looked less Indian then, at least not like the native Mohawk of Kahnawake. Her eyes are hazel brown; her hair autumn colored, with a natural curl at the ends. It is genetically clear Sahra's unknown father not of *First Nation* blood.

Sahra Moon and Dani talk mostly about the past. They talk about patrons, who have disappeared since a long time, about last winter's snowstorm that trapped them in the bar well past closing, and about the changing facade along the Main. And as always they get into another conversation about politics: about the calculated practice of colonization in the past, about the fight for *First Nation Rights*, and about the political influence of the church on indigenous cultures. Not that Dani holds any solutions to these ever present resentments of past abuses. Dani is in fact an Atheist, seeing everything from the outside looking in, just always for the underdog. Even though not a drop of Indian blood flows through Dani's veins, she talks passionately about the injustice of *Wounded Knee* and how the Native populations in Canada need to rally together because of stronger legal treaties made with the French and English.

What Dani says makes sense, only little will change in Sahra's generation. Laws are made by men for men. And even though Dani was born an Intersex child and has chosen to live as a woman, there will always be that "Y" chromosome that makes a difference. Dani will never know completely what it means to feel as though some part always missing-- like a hole that cannot be filled-- or the profound emptiness felt after losing a child. Still Dani is a good person, better than most, even than a lot of women, who pretend friendship just so they can position themselves to take something. Sahra therefore agrees without contestation, saying only that maybe things might have been different had she been born all white.

However, deep down Sahra knows things more complicated than just this. She had grown up on Kahnawake, went to school there. Because she was prettier than most girls her age, Sahra got invited to parties, where she started drinking and getting passed around, Then one morning at the age of fifteen she wakes up pregnant. Not sure who the father, she wants to have an abortion. But her grandmother insists that this was not the Indian way, but the white man's way. Adding that if she were all Indian, Sahra would know this. Her mother chooses to remain silent on the issue, yielding guiltily to the influence of elder tradition. Sahra hated her mother for that-- hated her because presence of a father absent all her life. Nor was it the policy of tribal council to get involved in domestic decisions when it came to young pregnant girls. So she has a baby boy and names him James after her white father Sahra never knew. At least this was a white man's name. At least James might have a chance--a chance she never had.

On Sahra's eighteenth birthday she leaves the toddler in her mother's care and goes out on the town to celebrate.

A young woman needs to get out sometimes! She knew her mother drank and smoked too much, knew she was sometimes careless. An hour before closing time the Police find Sahra at the Come Back Inn and give her the tragic news.

"It's a shame no one on the reservation knew CPR," one of the officers says on the ride home. "Why would a mother leave her baby in the care of a drunken Indian?"

"Don't be so hard on her, Sam. She's just a young girl." The one driving rescues in an attempt to ease her guilt. "We all make mistakes. I 'm sorry Miss for your loss. At least your mother revived."

The Paramedics put on the death certificate: "*Cause of death by smoke inhalation.*" It makes little difference: her child dead and her Indian mother still alive! On the Reserve only the strong survive, guilt and forgiveness dispatched along with the weak. Sahra's mother dies six months later of hardened arteries. Sahra does not shed a tear; her heart empty, as at last she knows full meaning of the Indian way.

As usual, Sahra is weeping bitterly an hour later and demanding Dani buy her another shot of whiskey. Dani instructs Lou to pour one last on her tab. She knows the time for reminiscing over. Dani knows from experience that once Sahra slips down into the mire of self-loathing, the combination of guilt and alcohol destroys all further communication. Eighteen seasons have passed, and still the hatred remains, a necrotic wound that no amount of time or alcohol can heal. This is Sahra Moon's Indian side—the side that caused her to be self destructive. Her beauty unmasked, she becomes unpredictable and dangerous.

Sahra finds herself sprawled on the sidewalk in front of Chiron's Gate. Her knuckles bleeding, meaning she has either been in a fight, or else hit something hard with her fist. The last thing clear in Sahra's mind is Dani and the bartender ushering her out the door. Then a tall black man rushes to her rescue, pushing the other two aside. Sahra clutches the arm of her unknown benefactor and staggers along the sidewalk in his strong embrace. She only vaguely remembers passing through the arch of Chiron's Gate, and very little after that.

As though in a dream, she perceives the face of the Dancing Girl leaning over her. Then the vague recollection of a warm sweater slipped over her shivering body and a whispering in her ear.

"Sahra Moon, it is time to find your way back."

The taxi driver agrees to drop Sahra at entrance of the St-Laurent Railway Bridge connecting LaSalle to Kahnawake. He could have taken them by way of the Mercier, but refuses to cross over into the reservation at this hour. After brief negotiation in French a settlement of price reached. Sahra is not alone. The Dancing Girl from Chiron's Gate is with her willing to pay for the longer detour.

"Why are you here?" Sahra wants to know with a drunken slur.

"I am here for many reasons, but mostly because tonight you need me."

Sahra mumbles bitterly that she needs no one and wants no one.

"If that were true I would not be here."

"What makes you so special?" Sahra scoffs.

"I am not the one special."

The Dancing Girl gazes deeply into the woman's eyes, unblinking and without judgment. Sahra sees within the nadir of those eyes reflection of her own soul. A person of who once she was; but more she sees the person she has become. Sahra does not particularly like what she sees. With nothing else to say, she turns toward the side window and watches the city lights of Montreal fade into darkness.

"Nous sommes arrives," the driver announces huskily, and then disdainfully adds: "Vingt piece ma salops!"

It is the Dancing Girl who pays, gazing steadfastly into the rude fellow's eyes without animosity; but mostly without fear. She has known such men before; knows the terror of weakness they harbor within, and that given opportunity, all capable of being predators. He takes the money, hastily rolls-up the window, and locks the doors.

As the taxi speeds away, Sahra Moon viciously shouts obscenities, using her native tongue spoken on the reservation. This advocacy of defense is her way to have the last word. The only voice she has.

She and the Dancing Girl begin walking along the train track crossing the St-Laurent. Sahra stumbles, picks herself back up. This is not the first time she has walked the rails.

"Why are you still here?"

"I want to make sure you get to the other side."

"No-- it's more than that! You probably heard I'm easy and that if you give me something I will give you something back. Maybe you heard right. Even someone like you wants something--what is it that you really want?"

The Dancing Girl looks up at the moon that hangs full suspended over the Reservation of Kahnawake. Below churn waters of the St-Laurent, as they have churned long before Jacque Cartier sailed along the banks of territories belonging to nations of indigenous populations. This begins a pandering history of colonization, first by spoiling local customs, and then slow assimilation spawn by human greed cultivated from within and from without.

"I know it was a night like this that you lost your child."

"Who told you that?" Sahra lashes out. "You don't know anything about me. Everyone blames me--but it wasn't my fault!"

"No, it was not your fault."

"Then just go and leave me alone!"

"I can't go Sahra Moon. As I said, there is a reason why I am here."

Sahra wants to say something back, but finds no words to express really what she feels. It was eighteen years ago this night that she left her beautiful baby boy in the care of her mother. If only she had not gone out that night. If only her mother had not been an alcoholic Indian.

"It was the Indian way that killed my son!"

There--she said it! This is the source of all the anger and all the guilt since then. At last she placed the blame where it belongs. Blame is all she has left, the only thing that really matters.

"The pattern traversed less important, Sahra Moon, than the path taken to get there. The Indian way--the white man way--every way appears right at beginning, but all lead to the same end. But not every course is your course to take Sahra Moon."

"You sound too much like my grandmother. All she cares about is the old ways. She rejected her own daughter just because she married a white man! Rejected me--my white blood! I detest her for that. I hate her Indian blood! But I hate my mother even more because she is the one responsible! Had I been born a man, things might have turned out different. At least my son had chance in beginning for a better life-- *at least he might have escaped the Reservation!"*

"Even by law of the Indian way, there comes a season of harvest to all things. Believe more in the power of conditions you can change, than those elements you cannot. This is the only passage to true freedom."

Sahra begins cursing without really listening. She curses family and friends, people she has known that only wanted to use her and those that allowed her to use them. She curses authorities that she perceives as instruments of hypocritical society designed to keep her from having fun in life, and all the *Tricks* that pay her with candy instead of real money. Then she turns and looks into the Dancing Girl's calm eyes

"You are lost just like me-- *only you don't know it!"*

"You are wrong Sahra Moon. To hate anything is to hate your own reflection even more. The earth overflows with hate and fear, unseen tentacles which only get stronger through progressive history. There will come a day when hate and fear divides all. And in the end hate and fear will be all that's left and all that's real to this world. Now is the moment to become stronger than your hate, to unshackle the chains of your guilt. Remember prayers of your aunt that instructed you as a child. These are not words only, Sahra Moon."

Never has anyone spoken to Sahra like this before. It is as though a weight of darkness lifted from her heart. Yes, it is time... *time to let go.* Stepping onto the outer-ledge of the bridge, she spreads her arms to the spirits of her grandmother's ancestry, to the modern ways that drained love from her mother's eyes, and to promise of something better than found in ashes of remembered graves. In the distance Kahnawake beckons to some latent instinct of bloodline. Below flows darkly the primordial St-Laurent River, as a ribbon dividing many principalities; and suspended in the middle of a starry night sky glows silvery reflection of a full moon inviting rest to her weary soul at last.

"Let's fly together free Sahra Moon."

The Dancing Girl takes gently the Indian girl's hand. And Sahra Moon changes light as air.

"I forgive!" Sahra cries, leaping into the night. *"I forgive all!"*

The next morning two local SQ Officers find an Indian girl hanging from pylon of the bridge crossing into the Mohawk territory on the Châteauguay side. A miracle she was alive, a freak accident that the oversized sweater snagged on the sharp edge of a metal girder, suspending her weight through the night. In the distance, Sunday church bells begin knelling, as both men remark how peaceful Sahra's countenance. Her face washed clean with tears.

Gingerly pulling the woman to safety, they place her in the backseat of their Police Cruiser. She claims there was someone else with her and that they jumped both together. Although there is no evidence of another soul, they make a search of the area anyway. Nor are they later able to confirm any records of a cab fare from the night before. The official report reads:

"With an alcohol count that high she might just as easily have seen Angels."

Nevertheless, there is no denying that Sahra Moon got here somehow, which continues to remain a mystery.

Sahra Moon vanished from Chiron's Gate after that night. Gossip at the Ziggurat is that she stopped drinking and found God. She now stays on the Kahnawake Reserve where she started a Day Care Center to educate young Indian children about true ways of this world. These remain unverified, since all know that no one ever really escapes here alive.

Only the Dancing Girl certain about what really happened to Sahra Moon over Kahnawake that night. As forever she dances somewhere beyond the stars and keeps always these events secret in her heart.

10

Dream of Beauty

*"So she bites into the fruit
cursed by jealousy
and slumbers in illusion
of beauty's dream."*

*T*he anointed hero discovers gates of a hidden

kingdom lost in tangle of enchantment. Inside he finds
captains of the guards and handmaidens, gardeners and
huntsmen, carpenters and cooks --all asleep at their task.
There is a Hall of Audience where the King and his Queen

slumber peacefully upon royal thrones surrounded by unconscious attendants. Everything is as it may have been once upon a time long ago. But all those that sleep so soundly refuse to awaken, remaining unchanged since then: all as mockery of the living and testament of death everlasting. The very clothes they wear have resisted decay; not even the cobweb ceilings, or rich tapestries have faded in the least. It is as though everything attending the hour of resurrection.

Searching through musty catacombs that lace the castle walls, the valiant Prince comes to a door slightly ajar. Peering through the crack he sees within a sight that inspires new meaning to why he has braved the perils to come here. She lies in beautiful repose a bride prepared, as though she is sleeping like all the rest waiting to be awakened. Still clasped in her delicate fingers is a wooden spindle tipped with poison of a curse. Then he knows without really knowing why he has come. He knows he has been sent here by will of a greater command, and that there can be no other way. Throwing back the curtains he kneels beside presence of the Sleeping Beauty and tenderly kisses softness of her lips.

As the storybook reads Sleeping Beauty opens her eyes seeing her Prince Charming bending over, the dream-kiss still on his lips. After so very long, the Fairy Queen's curse is ended, as the whole kingdom snaps instantly to life. The King and Queen resume their chatter where they had left off. The gardener goes out and begins tending his garden, the handmaid continues curling the Queen's hair, the guards jump to attention at the doors, and the huntsman resumes sharpening his arrows. All begins again as it had stopped when Beauty swooned under the curse: a curse so great that the entire kingdom succumbed with her into dreamless slumber. Dreamless, that is, until this new beginning. And the Prince and Princess gaze knowingly *into each other's eyes, made happy in the love at last they have found.*

"Here tomorrow," proclaims the King once he knows all the truth. "Our princess shall marry Charming, the Prince of her dream, who saves us all!"

And so the morrow comes and they are married in the Royal Garden which the gardener spent all night restoring. Beauty and her Prince Charming live happily ever after, which should have been end of this account. And surely there would be many fables born by sons and by daughters, each telling the tale in their own way. But had they known the whole truth about the Sleeping Beauty, it is certain the text would have been recorded in an even greater book. So begins here the rest of this story.

The fairytale book slips slowly from her hands. The sedative begins to work. It won't be long now. Her eyes too heavy to continue reading— almost she is in her dream. When next her eyes open, Venus will arise fully at last. Reflection of the person she has known always she was meant to be, but never fully embraced. The long awaited surgery scheduled for early next morning.

Before Venus, she was someone else, only can no longer remember that person. She has vague recollection of his eyes glimpsed in a mirror. The things he did and saw as a man of war! But that was long ago— long before she started to live. He is now buried in her heart, along with the pain; and knows peace at last. It is her time to know, to feel, and to be— this the true dawn of a new beginning!

Only now she is certain that it all matters little in the end, convinced that fairytale endings written just for children. This is the real world-- a place very different-- a place where everyone wears a mask and where faces reflect only half truth. At least now she knows the difference. Yes, at least her body will soon fit her mask!

She is only vaguely aware when the night nurse removes the book resting under her numb fingers. The sleeping beauty slumbers in forgetfulness.

Once upon a time through glass of a mirror Beauty awakens in the dream of another dream dreamed. And so begins beginning of this last story to end. Opening her eyes she beholds reflection in the looking glass the face of one familiar. She is naked, as always she knew she was meant to be naked, standing on crest of a purple hill mingled into fuse of golden sunflowers. Myriads of firefly planets bleed translucent through a velvet green arch overhead that promises more than light. Were she to remember seeing a sky before, the sight might have been even more spectacular.   Nevertheless, it is this instant a sight most magnificent, a radiant sapphire dome embedded with embers of glowing gems vaulting over this unreal world as the colorful canopy of a tent webbed with veins pulsating life. This is where she has always been; her dream already nearing the end.

The vision so overwhelms her heart with uncertainty-- such fear-- such joy-- Beauty begins to weep. She weeps for the knowledge of something she had not expected to find now-- because this dream is her own dream! A dream made even more wonderful than ever she could have dreamed alone. She does not know this the reason for her tears. Nor can she remember the meaning of tears before just now. Only something once crouched in memory that happened long ago, replaced by forgotten pain of something else. This present dream never thought possible, written in the topaz of her empty eyes, reflecting hope of a soul resurrected perfect from depth of despair into passage of this extraordinary new heaven. And this is the place Beauty's real dream meant to begin.

"What are you doing?" A voice enquires from nowhere.

"I don't know. Only it is new to me, because I can no longer remember when I did it last."

"Then why do it at all?"

Immediately her tears are gone. This seems surprising to her. Not because she is no longer crying, but because a voice beyond her own thoughts has spoken to her. For reasons she cannot explain she has known always that she was alone and never another soul able to penetrate the solitude.

"Who are you?" She demands looking around, expecting something terrible to leap suddenly at her.

"Who am I? Look up and Beauty will see."

Just above her head floats the couch of a lilac cloud with an elfish little man sitting robustly in the center dressed in gold clover.

"You are a queer one-- very queer indeed to ask who am I!" He sneers arrogantly.

She decides he is cute, more like a small animal than human, and could have been a cherub-faced little boy with green eyes that twinkle disarmingly, except for a long green beard that flows from his chin and hangs like dyed English Down over the edge of a waterfall.

"Well who are you?"

"You don't know who I am", the little man giggles and begins bouncing playfully on his cloud. "Then I will tell you. I am Me of course! Who else could I be?"

"But I mean who are you really?"

"I am really Me!" He remarks in disbelief. "And just who do you think you are?"

Had he said: I am not at all, that the voice you hear is really only your own mind speaking so not to be alone, then she would have smiled and thought nothing more about it. But to ask a riddle so profound that it seems the answer only solvable in a scheme more complex than what she knew.

Mask of Her Reflection in Venus

"This is all too silly! Of course I know that I have a name because it is only proper that everyone have one, and I am certain that I am a proper person. Yet, I can't remember, as though it contains a secret told to me a long time ago and I have forgotten the most important part of the meaning."

"It is obvious to me who you are;" the little man replies without sympathy. "You are you. Anyone can see it's plain. And you are here. Where else would you be? I am me, and we are here--how can there be anything more proper than that?"

Of course he is right. In some forgotten part of herself she knows he is right. But also doubts he could be altogether right. What he says made sense. Not the part about all things being somehow proper; rather, about it all being obvious. Everything is very obvious, only she cannot accept the simplicity so simply.

"Then where is here?"

"Why--here of course! He nearly screams leaping into a standing position. "Don't you know anything--anything at all?"

"No, I fear I know very little," she admits sadly. "I don't even know how I got here. Only I thought I was somewhere else, somewhere much different, but I can't seem to remember where or why I was ever there."

The little man begins pacing thoughtfully back and forth on his cloud.

"You don't know that you are you and that I am me. And that here is here," he ponders scratching his green beard.

Then his face brightens, as if struck by a revelation so rare that only someone with rare insight could have unraveled it.

"Of course there must be only one answer! Yes-- only one answer for all! Nothing is ever as complicated as it seems. For you there can be only one answer!"

"What is the answer?"

"No more questions. It is now time to know. Come--
follow me!" He then plops down into the soft center of his
cloud, looking decidedly certain.

"Please tell me what it is you know." She continues to
press as the cloud drifts away.

"You must be patient. Everything cannot be found in
one place. Come with me and somewhere else you will
find the answer."

Since there was nothing else to be done, she arises
and follows him. The grass pulsates sensuously beneath
her feet and between her toes sending delightful chills
through her whole body ending somewhere in her
stomach. It is as a lush carpet stretched into the horizon,
covering the hills, and flowing into distant lavender valleys.
She thinks the grass ought to be another color, but cannot
imagine what that color should be and therefore decides
the hue perfect for here.

Mountains teeter on the kaleidoscope skyline as
shimmering parasols balanced at the edge of the world
becoming a pattern more precise than the random
symmetry allowed by nature. Here are rich forests of giant
flowers sprouting from the ground, splashing vibrantly upon
palette of a landscape blended into a fuse. Shimmering
silver lakes and ribbons of gold rivers appear suspended
upon a near horizon that seems pieces of a puzzle
changing into sky. Then something materializes; a
phenomenon strange to even this place. It is as an
enormous pink halo scrolled from the heavens, vaulting
across the expanse like a ring of smoke sprinkled with
stars shedding glittering trails.

"What is that?"

The little man only yawns, continuing to lay mystically on
his cloud, as though in a trance oblivious to all.

"What is what?"

"It is as if part of the sky has broken off and moving
toward us!" She cries frantically pointing.

"The sky is as the sky should be. There is nothing new in the sky for me."

"Yes, I am sure you have seen it before, but to me it is mystery of something new. Please show just a little patience.

"Never a mystery was here."

"Since I don't even know where here is, then how can I know clearly anything else about here?"

"All is clear to her that sees clear." His tone changes reverent. "Beauty was, the world was, and always was here."

"Riddles -- riddles -- riddles -- why always riddles--don't you know anything else!"

As she speaks the energetic ring surrounds her, swarming as a myriad of insect creatures. They appear to have no substance, altogether transparent, made of pure light, showering her body in a stream of delicate crystals. Upon touching her flesh they dissolve away as snowflakes, melting into the tone of her skin. As quickly as it came, the grand halo begins moving away, continuing its odyssey across the psychedelic expanse, followed by a wake of shimmering living rain.

In frustration she plops down discouragingly on a pearl-white smooth rock.

"Ouch! --Get off me!"

"That tickles," she laughs leaping up.

"There is no pleasure in pain!"

"I am sorry, but really I didn't think you would mind," she apologizes. "Never would I expect to sit on a talking rock."

"You didn't think is obvious!"

"You see, I am not from here--at least I don't think I am! The little man said he would take me somewhere else. To where I don't know, only he said if I don't belong here then I must belong somewhere else. Although really I don't see how that could be."

"You see nothing that is obvious! I am where I have always been, but it is obvious that you did not see me!"

"But I did see you--I just didn't think you would mind."

"Matters worse, to matters worse!"

"That's not fair!"

"Obviously it is not fair!"

"What I meant to say is that it seemed to me you were something to sit on, at least it seemed natural to do so at the time."

"Matters worse, to matters worse!"

"If only you will listen, I'm certain I can explain--"

"It is obvious and the obvious needs no explanation!"

The rock's tone so final that she throws up her hands and prepares to depart.

"If you will not accept my apology then I shall leave you to your own obviousness and hope never to meet anything so rude as you again!"

"Yes she really must be going." The little man impatiently interjects.

"Go where? It is obvious that there is nowhere to go. She does not even know what she should know!" The conceded rock huffs with indignant candor.

"No, she does not know," agrees the little man, looking down from his floating cloud like a pious little church mouse perched on a moldy morsel of cheese.

"No I don't know! Please won't someone tell me where I am and what I am supposed to know?"

"You are where you are," replies the stoic rock.

"Well then tell me rock where are you?"

"I am where I have always been. This should be obvious to anyone! How could I possibly be anywhere else?"

"Enough of this," blurts-out the little man from his cloud. "To be here is simple enough and to be there is obvious, but somewhere else does this one belong."

"Yes, you are right," she agrees; "I need to know."

"Well then, come along! To spend too much time in one place takes you never to the end."

She follows what seems an eternity. Nothing much really changes. Never is she tired, or hungry, nor thirsty. Always she imagines she should be somewhere else, but cannot imagine where that might be. The cloud always floats the same distance in front of her, the grass the same hue as when she started. Not even the pattern of the landscape alters; the horizon always far away; pieces of the sky hauntingly near. Indeed here is a special place: a place without beginning and without end. It could just as easily be the interior of a gigantic egg ready to hatch--or perhaps it would never hatch at all. She does not think this really. Rather, it is a feeling, as an artist might feel the contour of a blank canvas instinctively feeling the proper colors to use. Or a writer the blank pages of a novel in anticipation of the right words to begin a story. Something else as well, something that gnaws silently within. What if she were lost in pages of a storybook, a story where she did not belong!

"I don't want to go any farther," she cries-out suddenly and begins cowering beside a small hedge.

"To know is to go," comforts the little man, peering over the edge of his cloud; "not to go is not to be. You are you; therefore you must go to know and to be."

"But what if I don't belong here at all?"

"Not to belong here is to belong somewhere else. Somewhere else you will know what you should know, but you cannot remain here."

"It's all so simple for you! --But I am less certain. First you said here is where I belong. Now you say that maybe I belong somewhere else. You said follow you and I would know everything, but I know no more now than when I first began."

"You are already before the beginning," he says looking past her, his eyes pulsating calmly. "Only at the beginning

will you know before. Look behind and you will see what is
to be."
    What she sees so terrible, so overwhelms her senses,
and is at the same time so very magnificent. A column of
twisting bronze flames spout from a burning molten pool,
shooting up a spout touching the sky. No--not touching the
sky--but touched by the sky, and becoming one with it! In
the hot center appears glowing cinders as celestial
spinning jewels, nine of which begin orbiting the bright
yellow passage. Strangely there is no heat even though
so near that she could reach out and touch them with one
of her delicate fingers.
    "Through there you must go to find the answer. For only
beyond will you know the answer," says the little man
reverently.
    "Then it is the end! Here I will remain!"
    She curls into a ball, buries her head between her
knees and begins rocking back and forth. Then something
wondrous happens. A melody begins to ebb from within
the burning passage, growing in measure, becoming a
familiar song she has heard before. Only she has no
memory of ever hearing music or voice of a song before
just now. The music seems to grow all around her,
through her, becoming lyrics mingled with her thoughts and
vanquishing all her fears.

> Beyond valley of the Shadow King
> This our song of love from the He
> Knew He the Beauty before time
> Made He the music and the rhyme
> Made He the wonder and the bliss
> Made He lightning with a kiss
> He and Beauty before creation born
> So their dreams might dream as one
> This is our song of love from the He
> Beyond valley of the Shadow King

The nurse makes the first nightly rounds of her shift, as she does every night to check on new patients. She knows from experience that the trauma different for each individual and that this the most important part on the road to recovery. She had once been on this ward as a patient, except her situation different. Her life changed completely by a drunk driver. Only twenty years old at the time, almost she died victim of a hit and run while crossing the street after leaving her favorite disco. The police put the incident down as a random crime, but she knows it was the same guy she rejected inside the bar. No one would listen, nor could she provide an adequate description. Never would she know the name or remember the face of the man that tried to kill her.

Everything changed for her that night. She still remembers vividly awakening on this very ward less beautiful, her dreams less real. It took two years just to be able to walk, and it would be long after that before she found courage to go dancing again. Pausing at the bedside of one patient she takes the pulse, followed by another shot of morphine. It is too early for this one to awake. She remarks how they are nearly the same age and could almost pass for sisters. She so reminds her of herself once upon a time. She is pretty, resting like a sleeping beauty, with the same color hair as her own, delicately built. She also remembers name of a book she fell asleep reading just the night before. At least she might do well as a new girl. Still, it is almost always pretty ones that have the most difficulty with reality of transition. It is after all the right of every girl to hope and to dream at least once in life. Who can say whose dreams more real, as long as they seem real in the moment?

"How lovely beyond must be to make a song so very perfect in my mind," Beauty sighs deeply.

"Song--I hear no song! Not now, nor ever have I heard anything like a song," the little man replies, then twists on his back and begins pulling playfully at his toes.

"Surely you heard!" She says dismayed. "The notes and meaning so clear that I doubt you could have missed it! It is a song about the he, who is beyond a valley ruled by presence of the Shadow King. It is not possible that I could have imagined it. Certainly you have heard about this before."

He only yawns, covers his face with both hands, and begins stretching, barely able to keep his eyes open.

"My world is here, my dream this cloud. I know nothing of beyond," he replies drowsily.

"How do I go beyond? I don't know where or how to go alone. Please you must come with me!"

"Beyond is always alone. There is no other way to beyond."

His eyes begin to close irresistibly, as though the strain of looking so far has made him exhausted. Slowly his cushioned pallet begins to float up and away.

"You mustn't go now! There is so much that I don't know, and unless you show me, I shall be lost. Please don't leave me now!"

"You know all that I am. My world is here, and that is all I have ever known. I cannot go ever to beyond."

She imagines an amber tear escape from one of his clear eyes, as the cloud continues to rise, floating ever higher, soon becoming lost in confusion of a heavenly configuration. Her sadness now replaced with joy of another song.

Beyond is a land that was here
Beyond is a sea forever near
Beyond is fire in sky that forever burns
Beyond is greater joy to be learned
Beyond is passage through mortal end

Mask of Her Reflection in Venus

Beyond is the shore where tomorrow begins
Beauty opens her eyes soon to see
And beyond awaits the He

The fire changes, becoming an intense winter blue passage. And within this passage circles host of tiny singing birds the size of insects with brass beaks and fluttering crimson wings harmonizing into the lyrics now she hears.

"So you are those voices in the music," she says comforted. "But can your lovely song tell me how to go from here to beyond?

The passage that burned now clear
Beauty must pass alone without fear
Close your eyes and wish to see
In a garden beyond stands the He

The birds immediately flutter away, vanishing into the void. Taking courage to follow them, she steps boldly through the blue passage. There is sensation of falling in the beginning, an anxiety that she has made an irreversible mistake. Then she begins to float, swept up into pleasant currents of warm air layered invisibly through this wilderness sky. Closing her eyes, Beauty rides these streams fantastic lasting forever. When next she looks again, the birds are gone along with their wonderful song. Gone, too, is the wondrous fire of a sky once remembered, and all that earth called here.

It is just past midnight and time for the nurse to make her second rounds. The "*Beauty Ward*", a reference of candor coined by the two male night Orderlies, is particularly quiet tonight. The thirty-five year old woman that had a double mastectomy just this afternoon is resting with dried tears in her eyes. To lose so much of what it means to be female at such an early age-- still it is better than the alternative. The one nearly killed by her enraged jealous husband keeps waking up and asking for water. At least she did not lose her right eye as the doctor first feared. This is the third victim of conjugal abuse this week. These days what was the world of men coming to! There is no predicting the roulette of nature, and less so the copiousness of human desires! The newest addition continues to sleep and to dream. If only she could warn her how different real life from dreams of fairytale. If only her eyes might see the things witnessed these many years working on this ward. But who knows if her dreams might turn out different-- who knows if her future might be any better or worse?

This is definitely someplace different. A place she thinks to have seen before, but from another point of view. She stands beneath the spreading umbrella of a flagellated, nearly translucent, mushroom growing slanted, casting a shadow over her. From the veined root flows rainbow beach of an island surrounded by crystal body of a vast sea radiating in all directions like sparkling spokes of a gigantic spinning wheel. Sand composing the shore vibrates excitedly, making her dizzy to look long at any one place. The horizon appears concave, drawn up, and blended into a rotating sky laden with billowing pink clouds. Her starting position is actually an emerald rock, fleshed with fine pastel granules that spread away in anticipation to every movement with organic intelligence. When she takes a step it parts, retreating swiftly antagonistic. If she steps right it parts left. If she steps left it parts right. Forward and it parts in the middle. Trying to scoop some of the living particles in her hands proves altogether futile to the point of agitation.
Abandoning the attempt, she further surveys the true state of her predicament. Every way the same, every

destination the same destination: all ways end on this changeling shore surrounded by crystal sea. With the realization that she is trapped and with nowhere to go, Beauty feels a sense of overwhelming despair. Then a melody barely audible, the words of a song just above a whisper made of neither silence nor sound, but with meaning made instantly clear to her understanding.

In time I am Forever Now
In time is Beauty that was before
In time is sand of shifting shore
In time a sky that grows ever near
In time a promise greater than fear
In time things made invisible to see
In time awaits dream of the He
In time I am the Forever Now

"Who sings so beautifully?" She inquires looking around. "Truth is always hiding somewhere, even if it is not always true."

"That which is not yet, cannot yet be. The truth is in the passage, not always what you think to see. If truth you seek, then in truth you will find the He!"

It is this pulsating mushroom that speaks to her now.

"Is there nothing which is as it appears to be?"

"I am as I appear to be," affirms the mushroom.

"At first I thought you were an ordinary mushroom like the kind I seem to remember from somewhere else. Now I believe you to be something more--or less --but cannot imagine how or why this should be!"

"Then you have knowledge, but not enough, and have yet more to believe."

"Yes... I fear there is much to this world new to me. Can you tell me, dear mushroom, is there more than time in sand, and more to whispers in the sea?"

"Beyond time and the sea stands the He."

187

"Yes the he. I have heard much about him, but know nothing more. You are most beautiful in this place. Are you dream of the he?"

She reaches out to touch the tumescent flesh of this grand presence, suddenly inviting to some unconscious part of her imagination. This act she does instinctively, responding to an emptiness of longing not known until just now.

"Stand back! The mystery of this passage leads nowhere" warns the mushroom. "I am only illusion of the He. He is the one you seek-- not me."

"Yes, all speak of the he," she quivers. "I have heard of him only in song, but also feel I have known him always, as though he sleeps in memory waiting to awake. It all sounds so real, and yet somehow can't be real! Dear mushroom, can you tell me nothing more?"

"He is the one that was before!
He is the key that unlocks the door!
He is the change above winged flight!
He is the image above the night!
He is the jewel in burning sky!
He is the reason to the why! "

"Then he is beyond this whispering sea?"
"He is the Beyond," replies the mushroom.
"I have no boat, nor made with wings, so tell me wise mushroom how do I get to the other side?"
"Beauty is the key: all things made possible to one that believes! This is the only way to Other Side. Look to where the sea divides, here you will see a way beyond me."
"Beyond-- beyond is always beyond-- but beyond where?
"Beyond begins and ends by Other Side."
"Then I will remain forever here!"

"You cannot be where you are not," replies the mushroom. "I am Forever Now. When once you have passed, you will remember me no more. I am not, never was, and will not be after. Beyond is his shadow upon the sea. Beyond awaits dream of the He. All is as it may not have been, and is forever now. Where the sea divides approaches shadow of Other Side."

She cannot tell where the sea divides, or if indeed where sea ends and sky begins.   Then, she sees something. At first, it appears as a spot only, changing into a fluttering shadow, as a black leaf swept in a turbulent wind. It grows larger and larger, finally coming to rest on the shore of shifting sand.

"I cannot go by this way!" She cries. "There is no boat, and I am more than shadow!"

"It is the passage not seen that crosses whispered silence of the sea. One foot must follow another. Other Side is the only way to Beyond. Close your eyes and count to three, where beginning ends, begins Beauty's dream with the He."

"Then this is goodbye," she sighs, looking longingly at the stoic mushroom.

"Time is Forever Now." She hears the mushroom say again.

Closing her eyes, she counts to three and boldly steps into the abyss of this bleak shadow parked on an emerald shore.

The night nurse studies the chart of each patient, mostly by habit, but more because of curiosity. It is the first time she has seen a case like this. Fighting back the urge to take a peak under the covers she continues her rounds. Another new one arrived just as her shift was beginning. According to the police report she was a hooker beaten nearly to death by her pimp. The guy must have been an animal judging by the damage. It seems he wanted to be sure this one never worked the same profession again. Returning to the bedside of *Sleeping Beauty* she wonders if this one really knows the dangers in being a woman. Still, the choice perplexes her. When she was a little girl her sisters and friends often taunted her for sometimes being a Tom Boy. But that was more of a reprieve, than change of identity. Never having a choice, she just always accepted being a woman, even embraces it sometimes. But what if she had been born like this one and had a choice? What would that choice have been? Tomorrow is her big day of awakening. It should be interesting to know what really she thinks-- or even if her thoughts are her own. To know if her new body fits the desires of her mind, or if all just the illusion of a fairytale dream told by someone else designed to keep all women placated-- to keep them under the thumb of a *testosterone-driven* society interested only in fantasy. It should be interesting if this girl has any appreciation of what it really means to be female in a world of men. Is she one to stand-up for equality, or just another willing to sell herself to the highest bidder?

Instantly Beauty arrives somewhere else, a place familiar, but not familiar. Rush of air swirls the long curls of her raven hair, and then moves sensuously as fingers along the naked contour of her body. There is no sea, no satin blue sky or pink clouds. Here a striated heaven shot-through with red streaks vaulting toward a darkened zenith. An eternity may have passed since departure from the emerald shore, the mushroom already a vague memory in her mind. Time had no dominion here, nothing changed since the beginning. She has passed across the Sea of Silence, and remembers only the sea and the silence. She tries to think, but cannot resurrect thoughts that so clearly she once had and claimed as her own. There is lingering sadness here, sadness from before, again the sense that she does not belong here or anywhere else. For reasons she does not understand Beauty begins to weep. Then she hears a mournful voice that seems to speak from within.

Riding on back of a silver wing
Beauty naked in Valley of Shadow King
Once Beyond on Shore of Tomorrow
Other Side the way of forgotten sorrow
The cloud and the sea born in her head
The dream of a mushroom in Beauty's bed
The sky a gift made of love from the start
The rainbow shore promise of his heart
The crystal sea a passage crossed in his eyes
The shadow that was fear made of many lies
Darkness changed light a scroll to end
Only the He born perfect among mortal men
Beauty the lock and He the key
Together joined forever to be

She beholds in the void a shimmering presence flashing toward her as lightning. It is in her mind an angel forged in fire, with the countenance of a man, and silver wings sprouting from strong shoulders. In a blink he lands mythically beside her, his eyes not eyes at all, but intense points of light as stars in a midnight sky.

"Are you the he?" She quivers.

"I am not He, but messenger sent by the Shadow King."

"I know nothing of this Shadow King. And even though I have never seen him, already he appears terrible in my mind. I was someplace else, only I can no longer remember. Can you tell me where now I am and if there is choice whether to go or whether to remain?"

"I am his wings to carry Beauty to Valley of Shadow King. This is all I am and all I am meant to be. The answer you seek lies beyond in presence of the He."

"Then to the Shadow King I must go."

His back is smooth and hard like polished ivory, his flesh warm and soothing. Arching up into the scarlet sky he navigates expertly as an elegant bird in flight. She soon realizes that the hue of the sky created by circling vortex of innumerable burning planetoids pulled into a bright center as hot cinders into mouth of a furnace. These glowing cinders change to embers of shadow, their substance consumed into a thick smoke of even deeper red. She imagines rivers of blood coursing in straight lines, racing backwards to finite point of an event that happened in the past. So overwhelming the feeling made through this vision, she closes her eyes and begins to pray silently.

When next she dares to open her eyes again she is alone in a grand hall laced with openings into catacomb passages, all ending here. It is as the ebon valley of a moist cavernous belly with sable pockets containing skeletons with life sucked out of all that ever was and would ever be. Even the slick appearance of boulders are as fresh bones; and a faint hissing noise escapes from deeper shadow, becoming in her imagination like winged snakes darting to and fro. The only way her mind capable to describe this place is point of finality.

"Who has crossed the way forgotten?"

It is a voice she has never heard before, making her knees weak with dread, and a sense of condemnation that make all excuses feeble in its presence.

"Speak! Who has come to seek audience in Valley of Shadow King?"

"I have been told that only here might I find the He." She trembles, barely able to talk.

"Beauty's Dream is the darkness; He the light. To know me is first to know meaning of the He."

"How can I know what I cannot see? I am lost in your shadow."

"I am the light surrounded in darkness to make blind those that see. Since beginning I Am. I was and will forever be. Beauty is the illusion shed in time to snare many-- all saved by promise of the He!"

"Then are you the he?" She braves to ask.

"Before a jewel shined in the sky...before a shade over the sea...before Beauty awakes on the shore...I am before the He."

This voice rumbles as an approaching tremor deep in the earth, becoming substance of a presence all around her, but never local to one place. It is in a way comforting, but also a spirit terrifying, existing as a statute absent of human affection.

"Is he, then, greater than you?"

"We are forever one," replies the King of Shadows. *"He is the soft against the hard, love hidden in the law, the dream dreamed of a dream dreamed beyond."*

"Is- is this place also the Beyond?"

"I am the first and the last! It is where all begin, only to become lost through deception! Once entered into this shadow, there is no beyond, except by promise of the He."

The siliceous walls begin to shake violently threatening collapse of this mountain domain. Precipitously the cavern roof fades into a panorama of bright spinning galaxies filled with myriads of burning suns. Surrounding each are embers of twinkling jewels. As this marvelous universe unfolds, bright specks of light reflect beneath canopy of spreading wings. The cavernous interior illuminates instantly into a jade heaven laced with gold and silver, sprinklings of jacinth, amethyst, and diamond clusters.

"To see Me is to know heart of the He. By Me is the He. And only by love of the He may Beauty behold Me."

A supreme body begins to appear, becoming everything. It is an omnipotent presence encompassing all that is and all that will ever be. Infinity is the only way to describe the monarch authority of this Shadow King. Where Beauty now stands is the heel of his footrest, the land of Here a mere trinket in his thoughts, the mushroom shore a withered memory, the Sea of Whispers a wishing well emptied of dreams.

"In me is promise of the He!"

The many heavens pass suddenly away. Only silence remains. She does not know if her eyes closed or opened; or if she is asleep or awake. She wonders within herself is this all part of her dream, or if her dream the dream of another yet to awaken. Then irresistible emptiness begins to overwhelm her thoughts, a feeling of being erased. Just when she is about to slip into oblivion another song fills the void.

> *We were the curse born of men*
> *We were the passage changed to wind*
> *We were-- never were-- will never be again*
> *We were the way meant to end*
> *We were the blood in the churning sea*
> *We were the darkness before the dream*
> *We were the way Beauty crossed to the He*
> *We were the first promise of Shadow King*

Her eyes open suddenly. It is early morning and nearly time for the doctor to make his rounds. He has given special instruction that the *Sleeping Beauty* be conscious when he arrives. The attending nurse professionally surrounds the bed with a curtain, while still gently nudging the confused patient.

"I've been having a most extraordinary dream."

"Well it's time now to awake from dreams. The doctor should be here within the hour. His strict instructions are that patient "*Venus*" be risen and bright by the time he gets here."

The two women exchange a few pleasantries and the nurse departs, her shift now ended until next evening. Several moments later another nurse, a young Latino girl, brings a basin of water, soap, and facecloths. The nurse thinks to herself that the lady's voice a little crackly, but almost perfect. No one would ever guess anything differently. An Orderly brings the new woman's choice of breakfast. He does not say anything, but keeps staring at her, as though he knows something he should not. Venus says nothing and waits.

"Good morning Venus. I trust you have remained pleasantly sedated these past 48 hours."

"Yes, doctor."

"Do you have any other discomfort beyond the pelvic area that should be addressed?"

"No. *Was*… was the operation a success?"

"Everything went just fine, Venus. I think you will be very happy with the cosmetic result."

"And what about pleasure...will I still have some feeling?"

"We did the best we can to retain the nerve endings. I think in time your body will approximate the same erogenous sensation as experienced by most women. First, you must just concentrate on proper rest and getting back on your feet. Another two days of observation and you should be ready to go home. Later this evening, our experienced Head Nurse here will instruct you on how to perform specific exercises to prevent infection and how to keep the canal open during the healing process."

"Thank you Doctor," she says tearfully. "This means so much to me."

"Allow me to be the first to congratulate you Venus on this momentous choice for a new life. I am certain it has been a difficult and often ambiguous journey since childhood. Now that you are old enough to know what you want and have made a choice, I think you have as much chance for future happiness as any of us can expect."

Once the doctor leaves she begins applying her makeup; and with the aid of another Orderly gets out of bed. It feels good to stand up again. The catheter is an annoying anchor, but at least she can stretch and move around. After lunch she again falls asleep and dreams.

He stands naked in a garden. He is beautiful, as the innocence of a newborn child, with flesh made of moon drops mixed with pearl and hair as halo of a crown. He remains motionless, does not speak, watching her only through clear eyes that sparkle as stars winking through the eons since beginning. There are no words to express the measure of this moment. In this singularity of eternity she feels the emptiness of time and what it has meant always to be alone and separate.

"You are the He!" She weeps joyfully.

"I am the He. You the Beauty from beginning meant to be."

His voice is living water reviving completely her perished soul. He is the one always she has searched for. Only now does Beauty begin to blossom in greater meaning of the He.

"I once thought to reach up and touch the sky because it so wonderful and bright, thinking to find you in those heavens. But I could not see you there. I thought to understand you through logic of many discourses, only to learn silly fables. But your voice I could not hear there. I thought you the flesh of a sensuous Mushroom, whose shadow promised only a moment of pleasure. Yet I could not feel your love there. I thought you to be thunder in the temple valley surrounding terrible omnipotence of a Shadow King. And still I could not know your meaning there. Only now is reason to the why made clear."

Mask of Her Reflection in Venus

"Yes I have existed always in all those places, always a reflection reflected in you. Only you could not see me then. I am light in heaven. I am wisdom in logic. I am fulfillment in desire. I am commandment of the Shadow King. You are the soul and I the spirit. It is time to awaken from this dream forever with a kiss."

As their lips touch, Beauty opens her eyes to the greatest joy of being— reborn free at last! She has found the greatest measure of love always she dreamed to know. And this love will never change, nor forsake her.

"So Sleeping Beauty decides finally to awake," the nurse says, just finished taking her vitals. "It must have been a very sad dream the way you were crying."

"No. It was a most wonderful dream. Now I understand everything."

"That must be one heck of a reverie to make you understand everything!"

The nurse looks uncomfortably away, avoiding eye contact. She does not really know what more to say. She has watched this new woman sleep in dream; and now she dreams awake. Will her future dreams bring happiness in illusion or sadness in being?

"I know you feel a little ambivalent about someone like me. I get that from a lot of people since being here. You all know my chart and word goes around. I can't say as I blame you really. But don't worry I am use to it now. After nearly half a century you get used to a lot of things."

"Since you have brought up the subject… Yes, I'm curious why after this long you would wish to go all the way? By now you surly realize that life has no fairytale endings. Being a woman at any age is not always an easy road."

"This I have known since a very long time. One thing I have learned is that life is a string of the choices we make. This is my choice."

"I am sorry. I do not wish to make you more uncomfortable than already you must feel. My name is Eve. Please, don't take my remarks in the wrong way. It is just… I have never met anyone like you before."

"So you are an original flower blossomed from the garden, the truest definition of life."

The two women laugh reticently, each comprehending greater meaning to the statement.

"I've been working on this ward for more than 10 years. The things I have seen. Young pregnant girls stalked by enraged lovers, women with children and nowhere to go, and some beaten to a pulp because of jealousy. Women butchered by surgeons to remove cancers, others that change their bodies out of vanity, just because of some guy's fantasy. And so many in this world that never had a chance to know what really they wanted in the first place. Yet, you choose to be here, to make yourself subject to the animal mentality of this world."

"I was born unique and have always known I am unique. The medical decision then was that I might be happier for conventional reasons. So I lived as a boy and grew into manhood. At seventeen I joined the United States Marine Corps, and went to war. I learned how to fight and to kill, losing my soul through the passage. In life I have loved and been loved, but always I knew her to be inside. Always she wanted to live too. But even she is not the end, as you might reason; but only beginning of something more meaningful. Venus is me transformed."

"I fail to understand how choosing to live the rest of your life as a woman changes anything. If I were given the same choice, I think I might choose differently. I would make all those men pay for their violent crimes against women."

"Then you would only be another violence justified to commit violence. By end only the violence remembered, and only violence that will remain. I have been shown another way. Mechanical existence is a passage, not the end. We all have a choice, if only we might see beyond challenge of the moment. If *counting among the sheep* the way to embrace peace, then this is choice I make freely and without expectation."

It perplexes Eve that someone so lovely should also prove to be wise. She had not expected this. Then she realizes it not outward beauty she perceives, but the beauty of peace within. Yes, Eve likes this new kind of woman named Venus, likes the way she thinks, likes her for who and what she truly is.

"What do you mean by the phrase '*counting among the sheep*'? It sounds somewhat condescending."

"It is from a poem once written, but not at all meant to be condescending. In my way of thinking *sheep and wolves*, *he and she*, *we and they* are all masks worn as facades of distraction. Even a fairytale has more profound meaning than the inscribed text, if only one might perceive with the heart what the mind refuses to understand."

"I love that. Are you able to recite this poem?"

In nadir circumference of her sister's tired eyes, Venus sees painted reflection of a fleeting mask. It is her now reborn. Here hope of a better seed planted waiting for just the right time of watering.

Can you never know a wolf
Until you have counted among the wolves
Sat at council rock of the tomb
Howled a pack at silvery moon
Stepped silent while shepherds sleep
As shadows count among the sheep

Can you never know a sheep

Until you have counted among the sheep
Surrendered love to Prince of Light
Seen visions blind to eye of night
At peace to sound of approaching feet
As wolves count among the sheep

So begins rooted meaning of a new love story reflected
in an ever changing chronicle never meant to be

The End

www.ingramcontent.com/pod-product-compliance
Lightning Source LLC
Chambersburg PA
CBHW072129300726

48975CB00003B/982